The New St. Petersburg

The First Five Years: 1991-1996

The New St. Petersburg

The First Five Years: 1991-1996

John Slade

WOODGATE INTERNATIONAL
P.O. Box 190
Woodgate, New York 13494

315-392-4508

INTRODUCTION

In 1991, the Soviet Union collapsed; and in 1991, the new Russia opened her doors to the world. Throughout my lifetime, the Soviet Union and the United States had held a nuclear knife at each other's throats. Now, as an English teacher working in Norway, I had the opportunity to cross the border into the vast and mysterious country next door.

My colleagues and I at the Bodø Graduate School of Business developed a program of business courses, including Business English, at Baltic State Technical University in St. Petersburg. Between October, 1991 and May, 1995, Norway enabled me to make a dozen short teaching trips to both Murmansk and St. Petersburg. In order to learn about the full range of English instruction, I volunteered in kindergartens, grade schools and high schools, as well as in adult education classes during the evenings. Thus I worked with five-year-olds learning their first words in English, and with advanced university students who were reading Faulkner.

I enjoyed my Russian students so much that I took a sabbatical from Norway, and taught for the full 1995/96 year in St. Petersburg. After twenty-five years of teaching, that year in Russia was the mountain peak of my career.

Upon returning to the United States, I have been struck by the disparity between American newspaper accounts of politics, corruption and war in Russia, and what is really happening in the day-to-day lives of the Russian people. Our press focuses eagerly on all the bad news, while barely mentioning the millions of hard-working citizens who are creating new businesses and building new lives. The squabbles in the Kremlin are as ancient as the Kremlin itself; let us turn our attention to a far more important drama: the enormous struggle and tenuous success of a people who have learned to rely solely upon themselves. How do they live, those Russians on the other side of the planet? Ten years ago, they feared and hated us as much as we feared and hated them.

Today, they wish much the same as we Americans wished during the depths of our Depression.

Never before in Russian-American relations, from the days of George Washington and Catherine the Great to the handshake between Gorbachev and Reagan, have the Russians offered to the Americans such a genuine desire for friendship and cooperation. Now is our opportunity, after half a century at the brink of Mutual Assured Destruction, to work together, to learn from each other, and to build a truly solid foundation of peace. But since 1991, it appears we have made little progress. From the Russian point of view, most Americans have not offered a helping hand, but a meddling hand, and beyond that, indifference. Government-to-government programs have faltered; what we have not tried yet, beyond a few minimal efforts, are people-to-people programs.

So let me introduce you to the Russian people.

I would like to focus in the first three chapters on the Russian children, for their experiences provide an honest portrait of the world they live in. And they, not us, will be the people our own children must learn to live with in tomorrow's world.

Subsequent chapters will visit the marketplace, the homes, the parks, and the newly-opened churches in St. Petersburg, enabling the reader to become acquainted with daily life as most people experience it.

Founded in 1703 by Peter the Great, the city has been called St. Petersburg, Petrograd, Leningrad, and now, since 1991, St. Petersburg again. A person walking along the embankment beside the Neva River can step on the very stones that the tzars once stepped on, as did Pushkin, Dostoevsky, Lenin, Trotsky, and Stalin. St. Petersburg has been history's stage, and continues to be so today.

Step into history. And step as well into the future, waiting for us, together, to build it.

This book is dedicated to

VLADISLAV LISTYEV

a Russian journalist who was shot to death
in Moscow on March 1, 1995,
because he spoke the truth to his people,

and to

GALINA STAROVOITOVA

a Russian defender of democracy
who was shot to death in St. Petersburg
in November, 1998,
because she believed in her people.

Tusen takk (a thousand thanks)

and

Spah-SEE-bah bol-SHOY (a *big* thank you)

To the Bodø Graduate School of Business, and the generous people of Norway, for enabling me to help them build their excellent exchange program during 1991 to 1996;

And to my students and colleagues at Baltic State Technical University in St. Petersburg, for their hard work and warm hearts, for their courage and determination.

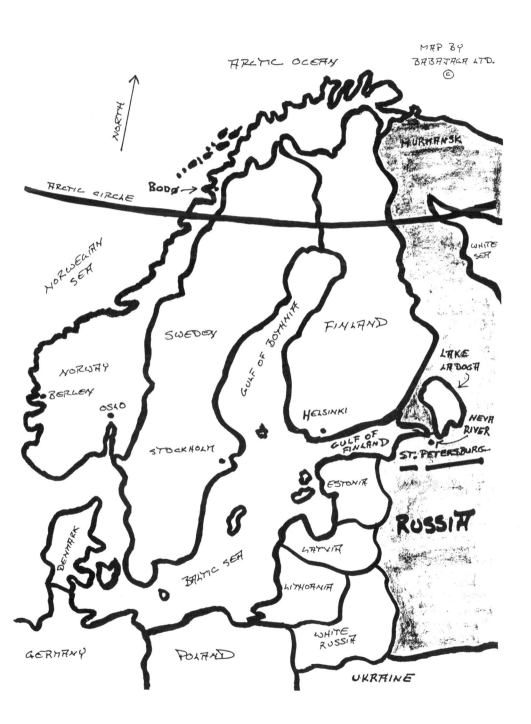

I offer this book not as the Truth, but as one visitor's personal response to the complex, struggling, warm-hearted people whom I met in St. Petersburg, a city of palaces and apartment buildings, of restored cathedrals and bankrupt factories, of elegant bridges and battered playgrounds, founded three hundred years ago by Peter the Great on the banks of the Neva River, and courageously rebuilding itself today, in complex, eternal Russia.

Chapter One

A RUSSIAN BIRTHDAY PARTY

On my first teaching trip to St. Petersburg, in October, 1991, a few months after the attempted coup in Moscow, I approached every opportunity with a mix of eagerness and apprehension. Yes, I wanted to meet the intriguing Russians, but no, I did not want to be mugged at knife point, nor caught between the barricades of a civil war.

Tatiana, our Intourist guide on the bus to museums and cathedrals, invited me to a birthday party for a ten-year-old girl. I was lodging with my Norwegian colleagues at a hotel filled with Westerners, and thus was glad for the opportunity to see a bit of "the real Russia". I felt I could trust Tatiana. Balancing curiosity with wariness, I accepted her invitation.

In the chilly darkness of a late October afternoon, Tanya and I shouldered our way into a battered, unheated trolley car jammed with people. Leaving behind the familiar territory of my hotel and the park nearby where I had been jogging, we rattled along a dimly lit street, turning corners again and again like a mouse in a maze, until we entered a neighborhood where the rundown apartment buildings looked to my Midwestern eyes as if they had been transplanted from the slums of South Chicago. There seemed to be an awful lot of trash and rubble lying around. Peering through the trolley's dirty windows, I was shocked to see children playing around a bonfire of burning trash.

"This is our stop," said Tanya, pushing her way through the tightly packed people toward the trolley's door. 'You're kidding,' I thought with prickles of apprehension. For a moment I hesitated; surely the trolley would follow a loop, taking me back to the hotel. A bit of sight-seeing, and then safely home.

But I hadn't come to Russia to spend my free time writing post-cards. Nudging my way toward the door, I once again placed my trust in Tanya. She had guided our group through the Hermitage and several

1

cathedrals; surely she wasn't about to lead me into an ambush.

We waited for the trolley doors to open, (a man had to push the folding doors open,) then we stepped down onto broken pavement. I glanced around the intersection, but saw no street signs, no clear landmarks, just a lot of people crowding around vendors who were selling things from tables and upturned boxes along the street.

I followed Tanya past a playground where the swings were missing their boards; frayed ropes dangled from a rusty, twisted frame. A board was missing from a wooden slide, so that a child's foot could easily fall through the long narrow hole. A small playhouse, painted years ago with bright colors, looked as if a truck had backed into it, tearing away part of its little roof. And everywhere there was trash: broken bricks, car tires, muddy newspapers, cigarette butts.

Scornful of the apparent lack of parental concern, I wondered, 'Why don't they get out here on a Saturday afternoon and fix this place up?'

We followed a muddy path through a maze of concrete tenement buildings, all constructed in the same style, Communist shabby. Only the large black numbers on their corners distinguished one gray building from another. We waded through paper-strewn puddles; someone had laid down boards torn from a nearby fence, so the water in the puddles was only an inch deep.

Tanya turned onto one of the dozens of identical sidewalks, then led me up a block of concrete steps to a steel door covered with Cyrillic graffiti. I felt increasingly uneasy, for never, especially at night, would I be able to find my way back to that trolley stop.

She pulled the heavy door open. It had no latch, no lock. Again, I almost refused to follow her; if I insisted, she would no doubt take me back to the trolley, to the hotel. But again, I mustered my courage, and stepped behind her into a damp-smelling entryway lit by a distant streetlamp outside. When the door banged shut, the hall became appallingly dark.

"Where's the light switch?" I asked, my voice demanding an end to this nonsense. Glancing left and right, I was ready to fight my way back out the door should anyone try to jump me.

"The bulb has burned out," answered Tanya's tired voice. She took hold of my hand. "Walk toward the stairs."

The stairs? Yes, now I could vaguely discern concrete steps ahead of us. As I accompanied Tanya up several flights, the smells of various dinners assured me that people actually lived here. The steps, covered with countless cigarette butts, became increasingly lit by a grey glow, for a lone bare bulb was screwed into the ceiling of the third landing. The steps up to the fourth and fifth landings, however, became progressively dimmer.

Were we really on our way to a little girl's birthday party?

Now along a brightening hallway we walked, past battered mailboxes and profanity scrawled on the wall in English. At the end of the corridor, a florescent tube dimly flickered. The parallel tube was dead. Tanya pushed the button of a doorbell beside the steel door. After a short wait, the glass peephole darkened and a voice called out something in Russian. My guide called back with a mixture of friendship and relief, "Tanya." I heard two heavy locks turned, then a bolt was slid free. The thick steel door swung open and we were greeted by a smiling, well-dressed woman, evidently the mother of the birthday girl.

I now experienced, for the first of many times over the next five years, the extraordinary difference in St. Petersburg between outside and inside. Outside, the once-beautiful city looks sadly dilapidated. But upon entering a home, even if it is no larger than a room or two, one discovers an entirely different world. Energetic people are bustling about; the furniture is neatly arranged, even in cramped quarters; books fill the shelves, books are stacked on the floor, books are piled in boxes along a wall. And somewhere nearby, almost inevitably, either in this room or the next, a piano stands against a wall, with sheet music open above the yellowed keys. Outside, St. Petersburg is a shabby embarrassment. But inside, the rooms are filled with warmth, light and purpose.

After meeting Svetlana, our hostess, and taking off my coat and boots, (Svetlana provided me with a pair of slippers,) I peered into the small living room. It was crowded with girls wearing bright party dresses, boys wearing suits, and several mothers who glanced inquisitively at the visiting American. Svetlana called to her daughter, "Larisa." A girl in a pink dress with a white bow in her dark hair smiled from across the room, then she said in proud clear English, "Good evening."

"DOH-breh VYAY-chirh," I answered in my rudimentary Russian, with a slight bow.

Svetlana ushered me into her kitchen, where, since I was a man, I should join the gathered fathers. Thus I entered the Russian realm of thick cigarette smoke and ample vodka. Though I am an asthmatic who often opens a classroom window to let in some fresh air, and a milk drinker content with one social beer a year, I smiled bravely as gruff voices greeted me and Russian hands reached out to shake my hand. One of the fathers stood up and offered me his chair at the kitchen table.

I was welcomed with a toast to the American. My hesitant sipping from a shot glass of vodka provoked unconcealed laughter. Gestures around the table informed me that in Russia, one downs the whole glass at a toss. My glass was duly filled to the brim, then their toast was heartily repeated. Though I had not eaten anything since breakfast at the hotel, I downed my vodka at a toss. The roar of cheers assured me that I had mastered the initial step of cultural acclimation. My glass was immediately refilled. I was then offered a plate of my first food in ten hours: small brown wet wrinkled things, which Tanya later told me were pickled mushrooms.

One of the men spoke French, the language which had been my minor in college. Yuri, (a heart surgeon, as I later learned from Tanya,) served as my interpreter, enabling me to answer questions about my teaching in St. Petersburg, about my hotel, and about my family in America. As I described my parents and where they lived, I remembered that today was my mother's birthday. My unthinking announcement of that innocent fact prompted another round of brimming vodka glasses, and a toast, "To John's mother in Florida!" She would have greatly enjoyed such a rousing male tribute.

Closing my eyes and thinking hard, I managed to remember the Russian word for bread. When I asked Vladimir, the father of the birthday girl, whether he had any "khleb", he put his hand to his heart with a look of self-reproach. He plucked an empty plate from the table, cut a dozen slices of dark brown bread, then graciously set the plate in front of me. Devouring slice after slice of the bread which has enabled the Russian people to endure centuries of strife and upheaval, I was able to survive my initiation into Russian manhood.

Svetlana appeared at the kitchen door and announced something in Russian. The men stood up from their chairs. Rising as well on surprisingly steady feet, I moved with them into the living room, where we stood in a semicircular row behind the young mothers. To Tanya's inquiring eye, I nodded that I was doing fine. Everyone became quiet as Larisa in her pink dress sat on the piano bench. Her mother stood ready to turn the pages of music.

As a lad, I had attended several of my sister's piano recitals, so I now expected little more than a stiff-fingered march through "Twinkle, Twinkle Little Star".

For a long silent moment, Larisa arched her fingers over the keys . . . and then she launched into a piece of music with all the vigor and dexterity of a young Leonard Bernstein. She poured out melody and pounced on chords, leaned into the keyboard, sat up straight again. I was astonished that so much jubilant music could come from the small hands of a ten-year-old girl. And that such a rich sound could come from the ancient, dull black upright piano, which not only her mother but probably her grandmother had played as a girl. Straining to make out the name at the top of the sheet of music, I read for the first time in his own native alphabet, TCHAIKOVSKY.

When she had finished, Larisa smiled shyly at the applause, then she leapt into a second piece by a composer whose name I read in Cyrillic: MOZART. Larisa's hands scampered up and down the keyboard while her mother, reading the music with unwavering concentration, turned the pages. Vladimir, standing beside me, watched his daughter with fatherly pride.

Larisa was followed at the piano by four of her friends, three girls with bows in their hair, and a boy wearing a hand-knit brown sweater. Each of them, as they filled the room with Chopin and Mussorgsky and Beethoven, proved to be a serious young musician. I might well have been at a professional recital, rather than a birthday party.

Recalling the wreckage outside, the broken swings, the tumble-down playhouse, the ubiquitous trash, I began to understand the determination of these Russian parents and their children. Though the birthday guests would walk home tonight along that puddle-flooded path, through a maze of nearly identical concrete monoliths, they would take with them the vitality of music, the glow of friendship, and the satisfaction of solid, undeniable achievement in the coming generation.

Escorted by Tanya, I returned safely to my hotel. I found my colleagues sipping brandy in a neon-lit bar, where I ordered a microwave hamburger and a glass of orange juice. I told the assembled professors of marketing, accounting, and international trade that what we had seen this week from the windows of our Intourist bus—the dirty streets and dingy buildings along the route between our hotel and the university—did not represent the people who lived inside those buildings.

Inside a gray shabby shoe box was a pair of golden slippers, just waiting for the opportunity to dance.

TO BE A KID IN ST. PETERSBURG

On Saturday mornings, to earn a little extra cash, Tatiana gave English lessons to preschoolers. The parents of these five-year-olds hoped that a knowledge of English would one day enable their children to travel to foreign countries, to become exchange students in England or America, to work with a Western joint-venture company in Russia, or perhaps even to work with a company abroad. Peter the Great, who founded the city nearly three hundred years ago, and who imported scores of language teachers from Europe to instruct in his academies, would have agreed that English was one of the essential keys to a prosperous future.

As Tanya's guest from America, I stood beside her in front of a dozen wiggly preschoolers. "MinYA zahVOOT John," I told them. "My name is John." They stared at me with uncertainty, curiosity, apprehension.

I counted from one to five in my lumpalong Russian. Shyly, glancing at each other, the little twinklers began to giggle. Now I counted from one to five in clearly enunciated English. Silence. They glanced at their teacher for help.

"AhDYEEN," I said. Then I held up one finger. "Wwwoooonnnn."

Several small fingers popped up as a chorus of tiny voices repeated, "Wwwooonnnn."

"Da!" I exclaimed, exuberant. Sweeping two fingers toward them, I pronounced, with the wide eyes of an owl, "Twooooo."

"Twooooo!" they all chirped, poking the air with fingers spread in little V's.

"Thththrrrreeeee," I said, with three fingers up.

Holding their pinkies down with their thumbs, most of them managed to display three fingers while together they exclaimed jubilantly, "ThththrrrrEEEEEE!"

And so it went.

I noticed, however, a silent pair on a bench at the back of the small classroom. Before class had begun, the little girl had been so shy that she would not enter the room without her grandmother, (or great-grandmother, a short bent elderly woman who had probably been a child herself when Lenin overthrew the Tzar in 1917.) So the two of them, preschooler wearing a black bow in her blond hair, and *Babooshka* wearing a red wool scarf over her white hair, stepped cautiously together through the door and found a bench at the back of the room.

By the time I had reached "Fffiiiivvvve," the girl had not uttered a sound, but sat in petrified silence, her eyes watching, wary. Her great-grandmother, a good Soviet citizen in the presence, probably for the first time in her life, of an American, also sat in silence, staring straight ahead, her face expressionless, her eyes blank.

So I tried the colors, first in Russian, then in English.

I must explain that though the words brown and red and blue and white and green and black are all one-syllable words in English, they gallop off in Russian with more syllables than I could count. My poor tongue stumbles and bumbles, my glottis gulps, my lips never seem to find the second half of "kahRyEECHnyih-viee" (brown), and the sounds that tumble out are at best a vague approximation of the Russian pronunciation as Pushkin would have it. But never mind, I was close enough that my scholars burst into giggles, and even the stony pair on the bench at the back began to crack a smile.

When I switched from Russian to English, the twosome apparently felt that they couldn't do any worse than their hapless teacher, for they both found the courage to repeat after me, "Brrroooowwwnnnnn!"

Stalin might have scowled, but Peter would have been proud.

———————————

From Monday to Friday, Tatiana was a grade school English teacher; she worked as an Intourist guide so that she could supplement her salary of twenty-two dollars a month. Whenever I visited St. Petersburg, I balanced my classes at the university with classes at School Number Eleven, a combination grade school/high school where she taught.

In the autumn of 1992, I brought a box of children's stories in English for her fifth grade pupils. Since my visits were brief, a week in the fall and a week or two in the spring when I could get away from my regular job in Norway, our plan had three stages: I would introduce several of the storybooks during this week in October; Tanya would encourage her pupils to read them through the winter; and I would return in May to talk with the kids about their favorite stories. I wondered, as I carried the heavy box into her classroom and set it down on her large teacher's desk, how I could engender enough motivation in a group of ten-year-olds to carry them through the year.

About twenty boys and girls sat two-by-two at their desks, chatting in Russian and watching me closely. (An American in our classroom!) As I opened the lid of the box, Tanya was called to the door by another teacher. While they talked, I took out copies of *Sleeping Beauty, Robin Hood*, and other tales for young readers. I laid them on the desk, so that when class began, Tanya could pick them up one by one to show the children.

However, the fifth graders, polite but curious, made the first move. I was gradually surrounded by a ring of silent kids, hands at their sides, who peered over each other's shoulders to take a look at these books. Without uttering a word, they glanced up at me and asked with their eyes if they might pick up the books. "Yes, you are welcome," I said as I set the empty box on the floor.

With excited whispers, they each found a book and took it to their desks. When the bell rang and Tanya turned to her class, ready to introduce the visiting teacher from America, she discovered that she didn't have to. The room was silent; twenty kids were totally absorbed in their books. Not a laggard in the bunch. They were looking primarily at the pictures, of course, and often shared with their desk-mates a character who caught their fancy: Captain Hook on the deck of his pirate ship; the Prince hacking with his sword through the thorn bushes that surrounded Sleeping Beauty's castle; Black Beauty galloping across a flower-bright meadow.

As the minutes passed, I saw fingers moving slowly below sentences written in English. A girl whispered the words as she read to herself. A hand went up. Tanya walked down an aisle to a boy with a question. She quietly explained a difficult word. Nodding, the boy returned to Robin's first encounter in Sherwood Forest with Friar Tuck.

The following Saturday, Tanya and her seven-year-old son, Pavel, met me in front of the Finland Railroad Station, for we had planned to take a train to a village north of St. Petersburg. Our meeting point, (we had come on different Metros,) was a towering statue of Lenin in front of the station: wearing a heavy overcoat, Lenin stood with his arm outstretched to the masses, as he had appeared seventy-five years ago at the beginning of his Revolution. Like all visiting Americans, I had questions about him, but Tanya was in a hurry to buy our tickets.

As we entered the station, I spotted a vendor with bunches of bananas atop an upturned wooden crate. Though Tanya lived with her parents, the three adults together could not afford such a luxury as bananas. Before 1991, seventy percent of the workforce in St. Petersburg had worked in some field of military production; Tanya's mother and father had been electrical engineers in a military factory, designing navigational equipment for nuclear-powered (and -armed) submarines. In 1991, when the Soviet Union collapsed, most of the factories closed or greatly reduced production. Abruptly, hundreds of thousands of people in a city of five million were out of work, or they worked without any salary. As the Russian economy staggered, inflation reduced the value of the rouble, so that money which people had saved during the Soviet period now became all but worthless. Families which had been comfortable two years ago were now struggling to put a few potatoes on the dinner table.

Reaching for my wallet, thick with thousands of Russian roubles which I had bought for a few American dollars, I purchased a bunch of bananas, three of them for Pavel, Tanya and I as we rode the train, the rest for her parents at home.

We stood in line and bought our tickets. Then, with a few minutes to spare before we boarded the train, we looked at the old steam engine, on display in a glass case beside the main tracks, which had pulled Lenin's train from Finland into this station in 1917. While Pavel walked all the way around the engine, fascinated with its wheels and levers, I asked Tanya, "How do you explain Lenin to your son?"

She stared for a long moment, seeing neither me nor the engine, but the many overwhelming difficulties of her life. Finally she said, "That is a very complex question." Her voice was filled with exhaustion, just short of despair.

Stepping toward Pavel, who stood looking up at the engine's cab, she took his hand and led us through the bustling crowds to the platform. As we took our seats on the train, Pavel between us, she turned to me and added, "What can any Russian parent say today to her child, about the past, about the future?"

The overheated train pulled out of the station. We peeled our bananas and watched as factories, then summer cottages, and then a spruce forest swept past our window.

Pavel stood up, said "Excuse me" in English as he stepped in front of me, then he walked about ten feet up the aisle. As his mother and I watched, he broke his banana in two and offered its lower half, still wrapped in the peel, to a girl his age. The girl and her mother stared at him with surprise. The mother peered over her shoulder and saw that the boy was the son of a woman who was watching him with equal surprise.

The girl thanked Pavel and accepted his unexpected gift.

She began to peel her half of the banana. Pavel, holding a bare pointed piece of banana in his fingers, returned to his seat, then ate what was perhaps slightly less than half.

A CANDLE IN A CHURCH

If we travel by boat in a westerly direction from the port of St. Petersburg into the Gulf of Finland, we will arrive, after a voyage of sixteen miles, at the slender island of Kotlin. Because the island guards the sea gate to the city, it has been a naval base since the days of Peter the Great.

Clustered at one end of the island is the town of Kronstadt, a blend of old brick buildings and new commercial billboards. In the center of Kronstadt stand the ruins of what was once a church. The roof has fallen in, the tall windows are vacant, and the nave and elevated altar inside the brick walls are as overgrown with weeds and small trees as the rubble-filled churchyard outside. The church was once capped with onion domes, but the outer materials have fallen away, leaving onion-shaped iron frames rising eerily into the sky.

One might think that this church, a jagged empty hulk standing incongruously on the corner of two busy streets, in the midst of shops and apartment buildings, must have been destroyed by Nazi bombs during World War II. But no, the devastation has another cause. Like thousands of such relics throughout Russia, this church has simply rotted and collapsed because, for three-quarters of a century, its doors had been closed by the Soviet government. The severe winters and the storms off the sea left nothing but the walls of an above-the-earth tomb.

I was walking through the rubble and trash in the churchyard, looking for the right angle from which to photograph the church, when two boys appeared, apparently intrigued by a Westerner with a camera. They pointed up at one of the onion-shaped skeletons, through which we could see the clouds. Though I could not follow their rapid chatter in Russian, I realized that they wanted to climb up through the ruins to that dome, so I could take their picture up there. Shaking my head, I told them emphatically, "Nyet, nyet, nyet!" Surely the bricks would crumble and the boys would fall. It was a disaster waiting to happen.

Undeterred, they headed toward the back door of the church. I looked around for help: someone who could speak Russian, and stop the boys from risking their lives. A woman was hanging out laundry in a nearby yard. A man was leaning under the hood of his car, repairing the engine. In front of the church, a trolley rumbled past.

Still calling to me, the boys scampered up some old steps and disappeared through the gaping ruin of a door. Though I could no longer see them, I could hear their voices through the weed-filled windows, rising higher and higher in the derelict church. Cringing with fright, I waited for a sudden scream.

Better just to leave. I turned and hurried toward a gap in the iron fence around the churchyard, where the rusty bars had been bent to make an oval space big enough for a person to step through. I would visit the town's park, then come back later to photograph the church.

At the gap in the fence, I discovered criss-crossing strands of barbed wire blocking my way.

The boys called down with two thin voices. Turning, I looked up and saw one of them climbing into the onion-shaped skeleton as if it were a playground jungle gym. Terrified of heights myself, I could hardly watch. They kept shouting and waving at me. The only way to quiet them was to raise my camera and take their picture.

So I did, focusing on two ten-year-olds who may never in their lives have attended a church service, but who had clearly climbed up and down countless times in the ruins of a church that had once been sacred to their grandparents. During the Soviet era, the priests who had conducted services here had probably been sent to Siberia, or shot, and anyone who had openly tried to keep the spark of religion alive had most likely been imprisoned as well. The wreckage which now filled the frame of my camera was the exterior image of a comparable wreckage inside the Russian soul. Those two boys never knew what they had lost.

CLICK.

I turned and hurried away through the weeds, this time toward the gap in the fence where I had entered. With relief, I stepped onto the sidewalk of a busy boulevard. I heard no screams behind me. But neither have I lost the image of those two urchins, perched like angels against the sky.

On Easter Sunday in April, 1993, Tanya and Pavel invited me to a service at a church in St. Petersburg which, newly restored, would be open for the first time since 1917. Tanya wanted me to see an Orthodox service, but even more, she wanted her son, for the first time in his life, to light a candle.

Smolenskaya Church, freshly painted robin's egg blue, its stately columns and trim painted white, stood in the middle of a large, long-neglected cemetery. As we walked with umbrellas on that drizzly day past countless overgrown graves, their stones tilted and often broken, the church appeared through the trees ahead of us like an oasis, beckoning all who wandered in that immense drab graveyard to approach, to enter, and to replenish the spirit.

We could not enter, however, but had to stand in a long line of umbrellas, for the church was so full that people could enter only as others trickled out. Shuffling slowly forward for half an hour, we could smell the wet earth beneath our feet: the snow had recently melted, and the multitude of boots churned up the fragrant soil.

Finally, folding our umbrellas and shuffling shoulder to shoulder through the entrance, (as so often in Russia, people squeezed in and out through the same narrow door,) we managed to enter the jammed church. Looking beyond the throng of tightly packed pilgrims in front of us, I could see a bearded priest wearing a white robe, and I could hear the words which two years ago he would have been forbidden to speak. The Easter morning congregation listened to their priest, crossed themselves as they prayed, and stared up at icons which for a lifetime had been hidden from their eyes.

I could smell incense, and the smoke of votive candles, and the wet wool of coats and scarves. Equally pungent, I could smell fresh paint.

People had brought slips of paper with names written on them:

relatives who had died, and whom they wished to be remembered. People entering the church reached over the shoulders of people in front of them and gave them the folded bits of paper. The lists of names were passed forward from hand to hand until they reached the priest, who read the names aloud in his prayers.

Tanya pushed forward ahead of Pavel, nudging through people as tightly packed as on the subway at rush hour. I tried to follow, but soon gave up. I could only watch, as her red scarf moved forward through the sea of heads and scarves, her son behind her sometimes visible, sometimes hidden, until they reached a stand of burning candles near the altar. I could not know, of course, what they thought and felt at that moment; I could only watch their faces in the glow of candlelight, Pavel's young face deeply serious as he touched the wick of his candle to the flame of another, and then stood his candle upright on a small spike; and Tanya's kerchief-wrapped face filled with serene satisfaction as she lit her candle from Pavel's flame.

On Sunday afternoon, at her family's Easter dinner, Tanya's gift to her mother and father, and especially to her elderly grandmother and aunt, was to tell them about lighting their two candles in the church.

One dark Sunday in December, 1994, when the wintry sky was overcast with thick gray clouds, I walked through a park of bare black trees that stood above a foot of fresh snow. Towering above the trees were the five gray-gold domes of Saint Nicholas Cathedral, atop which stood five dull gold crosses. With a photographer's patience, I circled several times from one end of the park to the other, until for a brief moment, the sun found a break in the clouds and shone through.

Taking off my knit wool hat, I entered the cathedral. Inside the vast, dim, chilly church, clustered in candlelight near the altar, a half-circle of young mothers faced a priest. Each mother held an infant in her arms, or held the hand of a child standing beside her. A slightly larger half-circle of fathers stood behind them.

As I quietly approached, I saw that the face of one mother was utterly blank, as blank as it might have been while she stood behind a counter of a shop selling liquor and cigarettes for ten hours a day, six days a week.

But when the priest, moving slowly in his black robe from child to child, baptised her infant son with a cross of water on his forehead, her face lit with a radiance that rivaled the glow of the five golden domes crowning the cathedral, and the crosses atop them, gleaming against the gray sky, when the winter sun briefly shone through a rift in the clouds.

––––––––––––––

Walking one afternoon along a street near the central post office, Tanya and I came upon a homemade wooden cross about four feet tall, standing on a crude concrete pedestal. A hand-painted sign at the foot of the cross stated that a church had once stood on this site, but that it had been demolished in 1929.

Behind the cross was a wall made of prefabricated sections of concrete. The huge gray slabs leaned apart from each other, some as if ready to fall flat on the street. Peering between them, we saw a large vacant lot filled with rubble and old machinery.

Apparently no one now had the money to rebuild the church. But someone had taken the initiative to announce that a church had once stood here.

As we continued our walk, Tanya reminded me that the destruction of the church by the Soviet government, though an unforgivable crime, was but a recent event in the long history of the Orthodox Church. "Russia became Christian in 988," she told me, "five hundred years before your country was discovered."

AN EVENING AT THE SYMPHONY

At a performance of Tchaikovsky's *First Piano Concerto*, I sat where I usually sit: near the front of Symphony Hall, and a little to the left of the central aisle, so I could watch the pianist's hands. Most people prefer to sit further back, where the sound is a better mix of piano and orchestra. But I love to watch those incredible hands at work. I like to see the grimace and determination on the maestro's face as he pounces on the next spectacular sequence of chords. And I want to hear even the faintest notes as they bounce at me from the uplifted sounding board.

While the first violinist was tuning the rest of the orchestra, I stood up and scanned the crowded hall behind me, where a few scattered latecomers were taking their seats. The teacher in me noted with satisfaction that, as was common in St. Petersburg, at least a quarter of the audience were children.

The lights dimmed; I turned around and sat down. The audience applauded as the conductor, Alexander Chernushenko, walked onto the stage, bowed to the audience, then took his place on his podium.

"Excuse me, excuse me." I turned to see a woman stepping awkwardly in front of people along our row. Suppressing an irritated scowl, I stood to let her pass by.

She sat down in her coat, leaving an empty seat between us. As the pianist himself now walked onto the stage and bowed to the applauding audience, the woman beckoned with her hand and a loud whisper to someone across the aisle and behind us. She kept beckoning, with increasing insistence.

I glared at her and silently scolded, Lady! Turn around and be quiet!

The pianist, a young man in a dark suit, sat on the bench facing his black Steinway. He had no sheet music; he was going to play the entire concerto from memory.

The applause began to diminish. The string section readied their bows.

Now a boy of about twelve, nicely dressed and profoundly embarrassed, muttered "Excuse me, excuse me" as he pushed his way in front of my knees. He sat beside his mother, his shoulders hunched with mortification.

Supremely satisfied, Mother patted his hand in his lap. Then she looked up at the young pianist, who sat with his eyes closed, his hands in his lap, in the now silent hall.

I mentally put on blinders and focused on the conductor as he raised his baton.

I don't know whether you have not only heard, but witnessed, Tchaikovsky's *First Piano Concerto*. If so, you have been taken to the extraordinary outer limit of human accomplishment. The hands of Vladimir Mishuk that night held me utterly entranced, while Tchaikovsky's music took hold of my soul and soared with it through realms of Russian passion. From the first determined chords, the piano asserts that it will prevail. The grip of deep suffering is ultimately sundered by thunderous cadences of exultation: suffering has been naught but the means to strength.

I never knew that a man's hands could move so fast, that they could command so much sound from so many keys, that they could pour out not a river but a torrent of chords so overwhelmingly powerful. The piano led the orchestra in a relentless drive toward the final irrepressible triumph.

Then, the pianist lifted his hands from the keyboard, lowered them to his lap. Following that moment of celestial silence, the audience roared with applause. The conductor beamed down from his podium at the pianist: They had done it! The young man stood beside his Steinway and bowed to the audience. His eyes were drawn to someone in the back of the hall who called out, "Bravo!"

I glanced at the boy and his mother beside me. Their faces were radiant as, clapping vigorously, they stared up at the man who stood fifteen feet from them. Mother and son spoke quickly with each other, their eyes never leaving the pianist as he reached down and received a bouquet of red roses from a teenage girl with a black velvet bow in her hair.

I walked beside the Fontanka River back to my apartment, unwilling to submit my triumphant mood to the stuffy, bustling underground world of the Metro.

Lying in my cold bed in the nearly freezing room, I could hear the usual medley of car alarms in the courtyard outside my window. Now someone was warming up a truck motor at 12:05 in the morning. The driver raced his ancient engine, pumping the pedal: a sustained roar rose and fell, crescendo and decrescendo, while a misfiring cylinder, exploding at irregular intervals, played a syncopated solo. The racket battered the windows of a thousand sleeping people . . . and continued for about as long as it takes to smoke a cigarette.

Finally the roar subsided, gears shifted, and with a guttural grunt, the truck rumbled out of the courtyard and into the street. It was an oversight, no doubt, that the driver had forgotten to orchestrate a dragging muffler.

Never mind. Tchaikovsky was still thundering inside me.

And somewhere in the city was a boy who understood more clearly tonight what it means to be Russian.

In an adjoining room, or perhaps in the same small bedroom, his mother was sleeping. Despite a rushed dinner, a long wait on a cold sidewalk for the trolley, and a crowd in the cloakroom, she had prevailed.

BRING YOUR HEART

Walking in the snow along the frozen Fontanka River on my way to the university, I met a boy who leaned against the embankment wall as he watched several mallards swimming in a wind-rippled pool of open water.

"Ducks," he said to me, guessing with a glance that I spoke English.

I did not know the word for 'ducks' in Russian, so lamely I said, pointing at the water, "VaDA."

"Water," he said matter-of-factly.

"Lyode," I said, pointing at the ice, quite pleased with myself.

"Ice," he said, quickly meeting the challenge.

"Most," I said, pronouncing the Russian 'o' carefully as I pointed at the old stone bridge with beautiful arches.

The boy stared at the bridge, unsure of the word in English.

I knelt and wrote the word in the snow, BRIDGE.

"Brrreedge," he said, rolling a Russian rrr, his European 'i' almost an eee.

"Bridge," I said, pronouncing the soft 'i' clearly and correctly.

"Boy!" he announced with a grin, pointing at himself. "Man," he stated next, pointing at me.

Before I could meet the challenge in Russian, he said brightly, "Good-bye!" Then he turned and hurried off across the bridge. On his black nylon backpack was the name of his hero in yellow Latin letters, BATMAN.

Bring your heart to Russia. Bring some books as well.

You can take home a beautiful red wool scarf and a set of hand-painted Matryoshka dolls. And you can take home as well, from this city of palaces and slums on the Neva, renewed faith in the resilient vitality of the human spirit.

Come on over. The kids are waiting to say hello.

Chapter Two

So far, we have been getting to know the youngest citizens of St. Petersburg. Now let us take a look at a special history lesson which involves both grade school and high school students, as well as a unique group of teachers.

WITH RUFFLES BETWEEN HER MEDALS

Students in St. Petersburg learn their history in a way that American students could well emulate: every January, they spend a day with genuine heroes.

During the Great Patriotic War, (World War II,) Hitler's army virtually surrounded Leningrad, as the city was called then. The Nazis starved the Russians through three long winters while they dropped artillery shells on factories, apartment buildings, museums, churches, schools, hospitals and marketplaces . . . day and night, day and night. For two and a half years, Soviets died sudden violent deaths in the trenches surrounding their city, or while walking down the street. For two and a half years, Soviets died slow, agonizing deaths, one starving family member at a time, in apartments so cold that corpses froze stiff in their beds.

Despite this siege of Biblical proportions, during which ten times as many people died than were lost in Hiroshima, the citizens of Leningrad never gave up. On the evening of August 9, 1942, the surviving members of the Leningrad orchestra performed a newly written symphony by Shostakovitch. From Philharmonic Hall, the *Seventh Symphony* was broadcast by radio to listeners throughout the Soviet Union, as well as to listeners in Europe and America. Leningrad thus announced to the world, "We are still alive."

On January 18, 1943, after 506 days of the blockade, Soviet troops finally broke through the Nazi lines: Hitler's army was pushed back enough that a single railroad track was opened, allowing food to enter the city.

But another year was required, until January 27, 1944, before the Red Army could drive the German army into a full retreat.

At eight p.m. on the evening of January 27, 1944, at the end of a 900-day siege, the sky above Leningrad was filled with fireworks. The survivors in the liberated city celebrated in the same way that Peter the Great had celebrated his victories over the Swedes: with cannons firing bursts of color into the Russian sky.

In January of 1993, on the forty-ninth anniversary, I met some of the heroes of the Siege of Leningrad. Every January, as an annual tradition, the schools throughout the city invite the veterans who live in the neighborhood to a program that honors them. As a visiting English teacher, I was fortunate to be present at School Number 141 on that special day.

In a gymnasium with rows of folding chairs facing a stage, a dozen people in their seventies, three of them women, sat in a somber cluster. These pensioners had fought on that savage day forty-nine years ago, when they began a march that did not stop until they had reached the Reichstag in Berlin. While the students quietly entered the gym and took their seats, my Russian colleague explained to me that because the students meet with these same veterans at least once a year, they become well acquainted with each other. Sadly, each year fewer veterans attended the program, for they were getting old and many had passed on.

The students had painted a backdrop behind the stage: a picture of a building in flames, with the word HET! (pronounced "Nyet!", "No!") written across it. The backdrop was fringed with painted icicles, and thus it represented both the fiery heat and the frigid cold that had turned Leningrad into an inner circle of hell.

The principal of the school, a gracious and energetic woman, welcomed the twelve veterans. She spoke of the city as "Leningrad", rather than "St. Petersburg" as it had become in 1991, for the city's defenders still knew and would always know their home as Leningrad.

A choir of grade school and high school students assembled on the stage and sang a medley of songs which had been popular fifty years ago, songs about war, about love, about the Motherland. A teenage boy with a guitar sang a passionate solo; he might have been an adolescent Dylan, singing in Russian. A ten-year-old girl recited a poem by one of

Russia's national poets. Though the poem was long, she did not recite by rote, but with fervor in her young voice. A mathematics teacher with a guitar now sang an old war song; many in the audience joined him. The final number was a ballad which the music teacher and her choir had written especially for this concert.

After the young performers had sat down in the front rows of the audience, a veteran with a fluffy gray beard and a chestful of medals walked to the foot of the stage. He expressed his gratitude to the students and their teachers. Then he read to them a poem which he had written, forty-nine years ago. His gestures were vehement, and his voice, though an old man's voice, was powerful enough to reach every corner of that gym. Halfway through the poem he closed his battered red notebook, for he knew the words by heart.

When he sat down, another man rose and walked slowly to the front. Leaning with both hands wrapped over the crook of his cane, he spoke about that ferocious day, half a century ago. He described the events that took place near the school, along the river, behind a factory, at a railroad station. The students knew these places; they could imagine the battles, the bombing, the wreckage, and the miracle of triumph as the blockade was finally broken.

While he spoke about commanders and regiments and planes in the sky on that distant January day, an old gentleman in the audience, with medals on his jacket, tilted back his head and listened with close concentration. Behind him, another veteran, a woman, stared down at the floor as if overwhelmed by her thoughts.

At the program's conclusion, the principal invited the twelve heroes to a lunch which some of the students had prepared in the school's kitchen.

The students of School Number 141 stood up from their seats, but they did not simply return to their classes. They knew these veterans, had met with them every year. Mingling with them now, little girls in bright sweaters, and lanky teenage boys in bluejeans, gathered around the cluster of veterans, to talk with them, to shake hands with them, to give them poems they had written, pictures they had painted, to hand them bouquets of red carnations. The children of Leningrad shared a few personal minutes with the men and woman who had once saved their city.

I was surprised when the principal invited me, as her guest from

America, to join the veterans for lunch. I hesitated, for who was I to sit with this group of soldiers who had struggled and endured and suffered more in one day of that barbaric war than I had in my entire lifetime? But when she walked me to the table at the other end of the gym, and introduced me to the veterans one by one, their warm smiles and ready handshakes reassured me that I was welcome.

We filled our plates with slices from a variety of Russian pies, still warm from the oven and deliciously fragrant. The woman who had been so lost in her thoughts during the program sat across a corner of the table from me. She stared at me with her dark eyes for a long moment, and then she began to speak. As my colleague translated for me, I learned that the last time the woman had been this close to an American was when she had fought her way from Leningrad to the Elbe River in Germany. She and her comrades had discovered American troops on the opposite shore. She was glad, she told me with a brightening smile in her eyes, to see an American again. Reaching across the corner of the table with a frail hand, she gripped my hand and welcomed me to her city.

I thanked her, and was about to ask her if she herself had reached Berlin, when she asked me what I was doing at this school.

I hesitated, unsure of my answer. What would she think of an American, from the country which for decades had threatened her country with nuclear devastation, teaching his foreign English to the young people of Russia? We had once been cordial allies, then fierce enemies; what were we now? Her dark eyes stared at me while she waited for my answer. I told her that I was visiting the school for a week to teach a course about American poetry. She nodded with approval. Again, I was welcome.

She wore a white blouse with a waterfall of ruffles at the neck, and a gray jacket with a blazon of medals beside each lapel. A Russian woman of seventy-five with ruffles between her medals, she was forever strong, forever feminine. I kept my eye on her during lunch. She enjoyed talking with her comrades around the table. Though her hair was steel gray and her face imparted the severity of an ancient soldier, she occasionally broke into a smile that revealed a deep and abiding happiness.

In America, after a banquet for elderly people, especially if it took place during the icy month of January, someone would have driven the guests-of-honor home. But this was St. Petersburg. Rare was the teacher who owned a car. And the school certainly had no funds to pay for taxis. I watched with sadness and with welling respect as those old heroes wrapped themselves in coats and scarves and set fur hats over their white hair, then stepped cautiously out the school's front door. The old warrior who had spoken so eloquently about that day forty-nine years ago, now steadied himself as best he could with the tip of his cane on uneven sheets of ice. These frail soldiers would make their way home across terrain as dangerous as a mine field: broken icy sidewalks, loose or missing manhole covers, drivers who honked but rarely slowed, no matter how old the pedestrian. These veterans would return to small cold apartments in a city which, half a century after they had completed their heroic job, could offer them few fresh vegetables, and fresh fruit only at impossible prices, and increasingly meager stocks of medicine.

They had broken the Nazi stranglehold on their city. But who today would break the stranglehold of poverty?

At eight p.m. that evening, I stood with Leningraders along the embankment of the frozen Neva as we watched the "salute" in honor of the breaking of the blockade. Pink, gold, scarlet and blue powder puffs lit the broad sheet of ice, and lit as well the uplifted faces of people still enduring difficult times. True, few now were actually starving, and only drunks in dark courtyards froze to death during the night.

But neither was anyone writing a heroic symphony.

THE "AUTHORS"

While teaching high school English at School Number 11, I asked for volunteers to participate in a special writing project. Rather than write a chatty letter to a pen pal in America, I was looking for students who would write a full essay about some aspect of their lives today in St. Petersburg. I had already contacted a high school class in Florida, and hoped that the American students would respond with equivalent essays about their own day-to-day lives. Thus the two groups could get to know each other much better than if they chatted about hobbies and rock stars.

Twenty-five Russian students volunteered, most of them sixteen years old. They worked on their essays, gave them to their English teachers to be corrected, then they rewrote them, paragraph by paragraph, until their sentences were almost perfect. On the day they presented me with their twenty-five polished essays, I was so proud of them that I assembled them together and took a picture of "The Authors".

I took the thick stack of essays back to my room so I could read them before I sent them on to Florida. Each essay was several pages long; some were typewritten, but most were carefully handwritten. Many were illustrated with pen-and-ink drawings, or watercolor paintings. Together, they formed a mosaic portrait of life for a teenager in St. Petersburg in 1992.

One girl, who liked to ride horses, wrote that because of the lack of feed and medications, several horses at a nearby stable had died. Another girl wrote that she and her brothers now had less time for schoolwork, because they spent their afternoons and evenings on the street, selling flowers. A boy regretted the recent abundance of books from the West which were now sold on the streets. Most of them were crime stories or pornography translated into Russian. He worried (this was the essay of a teenage boy!) that people would read these cheap books and forget about their own Russian writers.

Other essays were more positive. A boy wrote with excitement about the Russian soccer team which had done well against Western teams during a tournament in Europe. A girl wrote about rock musicians from many European countries who had visited Russia; her father had helped to organize a concert in St. Petersburg, and she had met some of the stars.

Several students wrote about the importance of the Bible, and of their Orthodox Church, during these years of uncertainty.

One girl, fourteen years old, composed a piece of music, and carefully wrote the notes on sheets of lined paper. She hoped that someone in America might play it on the piano.

I was overwhelmed by the quality of the writing, and by the honesty of these open, generous people. Not a word of bitterness, not a word of anger, and certainly not a word of superpower belligerence.

I sent the package of essays by registered air mail from Norway, and phoned the school in Florida two weeks later to be sure the box had arrived.

The authors at School Number 11 waited all year, until June. The students in Florida never replied.

One particular high school class lingers in my mind. As a translation exercise, we rendered an old Russian love song into English. One senior girl wrote the words in Russian on the blackboard, while another girl wrote the verses in English. The other students helped by calling out their suggestions. Several times they stopped to debate among themselves as to what was the right word or phrase.

As soon as the class had finished translating the song line for line, three girls sitting at the back of the room began to sing the old ballad in Russian, as perhaps their mothers or grandmothers had taught them. Other students joined in, including the boys who readily sang the bass.

'Don't ever lose that,' I thought, standing at one end of the blackboard. 'Don't ever lose those songs in your heart.'

Chapter Three

Let us move on now to Baltic State Technical University, where I taught English full-time during the 1995/96 year. My students were between seventeen and twenty years old, the majority from St. Petersburg, though some were from other regions of Russia.

THE HOUSE OF EVERLASTING FROST

Most countries need only one weather report. Russia needs two: How cold is it outside, and how cold is it inside?

The temperature outside on this evening of early February is -20° Celsius, or -4° Fahrenheit. Nippy, but not bad unless one lives in a poorly insulated apartment building with large drafty windows and a concrete slab floor. Although two small electric heaters are helping the all-but-worthless radiator, my room maintains an average temperature of 53° F. I have lived in the cocoon of my Norwegian sleeping bag for the past three months: I sit up in bed with the drawstring pulled tight beneath my arms and a wool knit hat on my head, as I correct student essays, prepare lesson plans, and read thick tomes of Russian history with fingers so cold I can barely turn the pages. Sitting in my sleeping bag on a chair at my desk, as if I wore a bulky strapless gown for a soirée at the North Pole, I type these paragraphs with frozen fingertips on frosty keys.

Having no radiator at all, my bathroom (at seat level) maintains a steady 49°. The temperature in the corridor of this old Intourist Hotel is also 49°. The sturdy Russians who use the converted hotel rooms as their business offices wear fur hats as they read their faxes.

However, the classrooms at Baltic State Technical University are even colder. When students enter the Soviet-era building from the blizzard howling down the boulevard outside, they simply brush the snow from their shoulders, then sit at their desks. In a classroom that has never been warmer than 46° all winter, coats, scarves and boots are as essential as a well-sharpened pencil. My loyal students keep their fingers tucked beneath their arms when they are not taking notes. Occasionally the low winter sun, pale apricot in the gray sky, peaks in through the dirty windows and lends a few photons of warmth. But when I teach evening classes to working adults, the blackboard is trimmed with icicles.

I ask and I ask and I ask, why, why, why, "Pah-chee-MOO?", but nobody knows why the University is so cold. The students, the teachers, the dean, the stern grandmother guarding the front door, they all respond with a Russian shrug, "That's the way it is." One student surmises that the University has no money to buy heating oil. Another, a bright, curly-haired girl who is forever optimistic, tells me that last November, when (at last!) the hot water was turned on to fill the radiators, a pipe burst in the physics department, flooding a classroom with rusty water. The entire system had to be turned off, and several days passed before the old pipe was replaced. Now, other pipes threaten to burst, so just enough warm water flows through the University to keep the system from freezing. "At least we have *some* heat," she smiles, her cheeks as pink as if she had been out ice skating.

In December, a pipe burst in the fourth-floor bathroom, (perhaps when a surge of steam hit a frozen joint.) The bathroom flooded, and then rusty water, along with most of the plaster ceiling, dribbled and shattered onto the bookshelves and desk in the third-floor office of the chairman of the Department of Foreign Languages (my boss). I was impressed, as I surveyed the soggy dictionary on her desk, by Natalia's courageous smile and restrained language. For she could have cursed in several of the European tongues.

The central office of the Department of Foreign Languages is heated, feebly, by an electric heater that was once used by Krushchev's mother. The heater's glowing red wire is coiled around a ceramic core, which is supported by a framework of rusted iron and tarnished tin. Frayed wires wrapped with bits of burnt tape sprout at both ends. Were an American fire inspector to walk into the room, he could identify every infraction in the book.

During the ten minutes between classes, our teachers hover around this heater with their trembling blue hands lowered to its red coil, as their ancestors two thousand years ago huddled around the dying coals of a campfire in the midst of a February blizzard.

WHOM DO YOU ADMIRE?

November 7, 1995.

Today is a national holiday, but few people are celebrating.

Seventy-eight years ago, on the evening of November 7, 1917, the warship *Aurora* steamed up the Neva River to a position from which it could aim its guns at the lit windows of the Winter Palace. Once the home of the tzars, the enormous ornate building was now the headquarters of Kerensky's Provisional government. At 9:45 p.m., in the darkness of a winter night, one of the *Aurora's* six-inch guns fired a blank shot. Hearing the signal, armed factory workers and sailors, led by Bolshevik Red Guards, entered the Palace, captured the tiny government, (Kerensky had already fled to the protection of the American Embassy,) and proclaimed that Russia would now be governed by representatives of the common people. Lenin became on that night, at the age of forty-seven, the iron-fisted leader of the largest country in the world.

Every year thereafter, the 7th of November had been celebrated as a national holiday . . . until recently. On September 5, 1991, after a tumultuous seventy-four years, the Union of Soviet Socialist Republics came to an end as the republics broke away from their domineering big brother. The Communist Party was whittled down to one contingent among many in the Parliament. So, what shall Russians do now on the anniversary of the Great November Revolution?

At Baltic State Technical University, a state-run school, the professors did not know at the end of October whether or not we would have classes on November 7th. Nobody in the administration had yet made a decision. One teacher stated angrily and openly that no one should celebrate, for the date was "the anniversary of a tragedy".

The dean finally sent down word that no classes would be held on Monday and Tuesday, the 6th and 7th. Faculty and students would make up the classes on Saturday and Sunday, the 4th and 5th. The University planned no special events. The city fathers decided that there would be no parade in St. Petersburg. People were left to do whatever they wanted, on the anniversary of a country that no longer existed.

On Friday, November 3rd, my students informed me, (not wanting me to waste my time,) that they certainly were not going to show up for classes on Saturday and Sunday. I would not see them again until the following Wednesday. So I asked them, as the perfect subject for a class discussion, what they planned to do on Tuesday the 7th.

They shrugged, stared down at their desks, said nothing. I asked, probing further, "Will you talk with your parents and your grandparents about the history of your country, about the present difficulties, about plans for the future?"

Dead silence in the room.

"Yes," said Dmitri, who was often the first to speak, "we sometimes talk about the past. But people are tired of discussing the present difficulties." He shrugged. "Why talk about it? No one can do anything about it. The economy is a wreck, and we're sick of politics."

The other students around the room murmured with agreement. "Russia doesn't need democracy," stated Nikolai. "Russia needs a strong leader who can tell the people what to do." Several students nodded in agreement with this traditional remedy for all of Russia's ills: the good tzar. He is the Russian messiah, and though he has not yet appeared, surely he will. In the meantime, why vote?

Baltic State Technical University, home of the Soviet space program, is the alma mater of several cosmonauts. The University still offers courses in space engineering, rocketry and advanced metallurgy, but the Russian space program now operates on a severely limited budget, and so does this government-run school.

The classroom in which I was teaching had not been cleaned for several years. Every chair was damaged, their seats torn and loose, their backs often missing. The desks were battered and wobbly. Broken chairs and desks, unusable even in this wreck of a classroom, had been heaped in the back of the room, along with shards of glass and remnants of electrical equipment, all of it thick with dust and waiting for someone to throw it away. The windows were filthy; the dusty curtains were torn and dangling. The language lab console at the front of the room was now merely broken parts of an old tape recorder. The students laughed at it as they played with its useless knobs. Only a few of the florescent lights worked, but better a dead tube than a flickering one. The linoleum floor was so worn that the padding beneath it protruded in big dirty clumps. As an asthmatic with allergies, I blew my nose and sneezed for nine months in that room.

Outside the Soviet windows, their frames stuffed with cotton against the winter wind, the brick shell of an adjoining wing of the University remained unfinished, most of its modern windows broken. A crane stood in the courtyard, rusting. Around it were rubble, trash, and corroding rocket parts.

The bathrooms, of the University that had once sent cosmonauts into orbit around the earth, were unspeakable, almost unusable.

So why should these students care about politics? Their university-educated parents, some of them graduates from this same school, had lost their jobs at the factories and institutes. Their once-proud city was now a shabby embarrassment. Their entire country had become a frightening, chaotic shambles, and they felt helpless. Their parents felt helpless. Their grandmothers were old and tired, for they had already been called upon, time and again, to save their country, and yet they had seen a lifetime of hard work and noble dreams destroyed.

No one wanted to talk about it. So I changed the lesson plan.

Turning to the blackboard, I erased yesterday's lesson with a damp rag, and then wrote with a stub of chalk, WHAT PERSON DO YOU MOST ADMIRE? I looked up "admire" in my English-Russian dictionary, then read the word in Russian as best I could pronounce it. For the first time that day, the gang grinned. Looking at my watch, I told them, "I would like you to write an essay in class. You have forty-five minutes."

Without hesitation, without a single shrug, twenty students, dressed in coats and scarves, opened their notebooks and set to work. Using worn, outdated, pocket-sized dictionaries, (not every student had one, so they passed a few battered relics back and forth between them,) these earnest seventeen-year-olds began to fill their pages with hesitant sentences and scratched-out words. Whispering, they helped each other to find the right word. I walked slowly past their desks, ready for questions, ready with encouragement.

Know it or not, like it or not, this was the generation with the weight of Russia's future on their shoulders. If their country was to build itself anew, if it was to join the other nations of the world as an economic and cultural equal, then they and they alone would have to do the building. The stumbling, bumbling government of former Communists wasn't going to do it. Their unemployed parents weren't going to do it. The Mafia and super-rich New Russians certainly weren't going to do it. These beautiful kids, sitting in a cold filthy room and writing in a foreign language, were Russia's only hope.

I walked slowly around a room filled with future founding fathers, and, I was equally certain, future founding mothers.

At the end of the period, I collected their essays. As always, most of my students said "Good-bye," often with a wave or a smile, as they left the room. They were diligent, and they were polite.

On Tuesday the 7th of November, 1995, the day of no parades, I sat bundled in my Norwegian sleeping bag at my desk and read 64 essays, from four different classes, about the people whom my students admired. I discovered, as I worked my way through that extraordinary stack of papers, that no one had written about Lenin, no one had written about Gorbachev, no one had written about Yeltsin. There was not a single essay about a politician.

Two students wrote about Peter the Great, who founded their city as Russia's first seaport. One boy wrote about Alexander Nevsky, who dealt with both the Swedes and the Tartar Mongols during the 1200's. Two students wrote about Andrei Sakharov, the physicist who openly criticized the war in Afghanistan, and who was consequently exiled to the town of Gorky.

Several students wrote about rock stars: Jim Morrison, Freddy Mercury, and the Beatles. They liked the lyrics about love, about freedom.

The great majority of students wrote, with deep feeling, about some member of their family. "I admire my mother because . . ." "I admire my grandfather who . . . " "My father is the person who that (now the teacher helps) whom I admire." One boy described his grandfather, who traveled as a young man from a village near the Ural Mountains to the city of Leningrad so that he could attend a university. He became a professor of space engineering and was very much admired by his colleagues.

One girl wrote about her mother, "who is not perfect," but who has traveled to many towns and cities in Russia, and who is always willing to help her.

That was the predominant theme of these essays: the person whom they admired, whether a relative or a close friend, was a person who was always ready to help. With advice, with a set of tools, with a helping hand. Katya, extremely shy in class, admitted that she did not know whom to write about, except perhaps her grandmother, who can no longer work at the factory. Her grandmother knew a lot about life, about people. She was gentle. Katya loved her very much.

Which brings us to the question: What are we in America doing to help?

My students were willing to reach out, eager to learn, ready to become friends. They wanted to explore new ideas, they wanted to explore the world. They were, in my twenty-five years of teaching, the most motivated and polite group of people I had ever worked with.

An entire generation of Russian students is eager to learn English, if the schools could manage to find an English teacher, and if the schools could manage to pay for the books. America has been offered a golden opportunity, at minimal expense, to build the foundation of friendship and prosperity with a country which, for centuries, has been either our dangerous enemy or our dubious friend.

And yet, during my five years of teaching in a number of schools, in both Murmansk and St. Petersburg, I have seen only a smattering of books, cassettes or other teaching materials from America. Norway provided the funding that enabled me to deliver $12,000 worth of books, mainly in business English, to several schools in Russia. But though I have knocked on the doors of many American universities, I haven't been offered as much as a single pocket dictionary.

In Russian school libraries, I found quantities of useless books, shipped over from America. A set of encyclopedias published in 1952, when Stalin was still alive, "donated" by a library in Ohio that was no doubt cleaning out its shelves. Outdated chemistry books, with notes scribbled in the margins. Single copies of Shakespeare, Hawthorne and Twain, good books, but useless in a classroom without a copy for each student. Twenty-five copies on a library shelf of a porno-action paperback that did not sell in the United States, so it was remaindered and then shipped to Russia as a tax write-off. Americans call it "humanitarian aid". Insulted Russians call it "junk".

When American companies set up offices in Russia, they need people who can speak both English and Russian, so they steal English teachers from the schools by offering them higher salaries. Time and again, school directors complained to me of losing their best language teachers to western corporations.

I saw a modern physics laboratory at the University, contributed by a German company. I spoke on a telephone connected to the Norwegian phone system. I spoke with teachers who had taken a month-long course in Finland. But I saw little help from America. The best students in the world ask to learn our language, and we respond by covering the city with a multitude of billboards, advertising, in English, MARLBORO and CAMEL and COKE.

We should be helping entrepreneurs to build their small businesses. We should be helping farmers to work their land more efficiently. We should be helping the few scattered ecologists to clean up the worst of the nightmare.

But above all, we should be helping the students to reach for their dreams. Because foremost among those dreams is the hope for stability, and prosperity, and peace.

During a late afternoon class, the orange sun shone over the city rooftops and through the classroom's dirty windows onto my notes on the blackboard, as we read Robert Frost. A friend had given me a book of Frost's poems in translation, English on the left page, Russian on the right. Sitting comfortably on the front of my teacher's desk, I read the original in English, while my students read the copies I had printed for them. Then we passed the book around, and they took turns reading the Russian version, and in some cases, two or three versions of a single poem.

My students were familiar with birch trees, frozen lakes, woods filling up with snow. St. Petersburg had many sad city lanes that a person could walk while becoming acquainted with the night. My students quickly saw the nuclear implications of "Fire and Ice". Their nation stood at a point where two roads diverge, and those fine young people had to choose the right path. And old Silas, who had come home to the farm with a promise to ditch the meadow: Yes, they could imagine an old peasant such as Silas in Russia.

I love to read aloud the poems of Robert Frost.

Never have I found a better audience than in the schools of St. Petersburg.

FINAL EXAM

My 64 students wrote a two-hour final exam covering all the literature we had read between September and May: stories, poems, a novel, chapters of American history, and articles from *The Economist*, as well as lessons in Business English, including import-and-export terminology, banking terminology, and how to write an international business letter. The students were required to write their examination answer in the form of a well-organized essay, with Title, Introduction, Body, and Conclusion, underlining the topic sentence in each paragraph.

Passing their dog-eared dictionaries back and forth, they wrote the first draft of their essays, and then rewrote them in final polished form. For two hours, they wrote their hearts out. I promised them that I would meet with them in a week, so that I could personally return their exams.

Usually at the end of a school year, (in Norway, in America,) I had to drag myself through the drudgery of reading a stack of final exams. I always returned them personally within one week, to those few students who bothered to show up. (They flocked instead to the computer print-out of their grades, posted on a wall.) Leaving most of the exams in a box outside my office door, I would depart from the college, drained and frazzled, and stagger home toward the salvation of summer vacation.

But as I read those sixty-four exams, written by the determined young men and women of St. Petersburg, I perked up, became interested, even excited. The gang had done a beautiful job! Good topic sentences, solid paragraphs, verbs in fairly good shape. They used lots of vocabulary words from the stories and articles. Best of all, they tackled their chosen questions on a personal level, so that each essay was unique, and from the heart. The conclusion at the end expressed their honest opinions, as I had asked.

In twenty-five years of teaching, never had I read such a batch of solid exams.

Sixty-three out of sixty-four students came to my classroom when I handed back their exams. The only exception was Anton, who was ill at home, and sent his apology. A friend said he would take Anton's paper to him.

As I praised them not only for their excellent essays, but for all the hard work they had done through the year, they smiled with quiet pride. They had developed their skills in English to an advanced level. Equally important, they now had the confidence to use what they had learned. Unlike the shy, frightened, silent youngsters they had been in the autumn, they were now young men and women who could speak to foreigners, who could write an application to an exchange program in England or America, and who could write an application to a joint venture company doing business in St. Petersburg. One day, as businessmen or engineers or perhaps even as politicians, they would attend conferences at which the common language was English. They might even present a paper in English to their international colleagues.

They could learn from the world, and the world could learn from them.

These great kids had finally enabled me to become the teacher I had always wanted to be. As they shook my hand and said good-bye, my heart smiled on each one of them.

THE NEXT RENAISSANCE

The people in Russia are struggling to rebuild their nation. In the midst of economic disintegration, they try to understand and implement the market system. Despite massive unemployment, they slowly convert antiquated factories, many of which once produced tanks and nuclear missiles, into clean, modern factories that produce civilian goods. The Russians are rewriting their entire code of law, starting with a new Constitution. They are learning about political debate and freedom of the press.

But at every turn, they confront the same corruption and violence that have plagued their country for decades. Old Communists still sit in government offices, while the Mafia controls the marketplace; the two often cooperate with brotherly teamwork. And the generals, never idle, must have their wars.

During the course of fifty years, from 1750 to 1800, our upstart, rough-and-ready nation slowly took shape under the guidance of the incendiary Samuel Adams, the legalistic John Adams, the pragmatic Ben Franklin, the selfless, indefatigable Washington, the financier Hamilton, the visionary Jefferson.

But Russia today, struggling to emerge in a much briefer time from her political dark ages, has few Founding Fathers. Nor does she have a virgin continent to work with; instead, she must build on a foundation of crumbling concrete.

So Americans read in their newspapers all the ominous news from Russia, while Russian children stumble on broken icy sidewalks toward their dark future.

I believe, however, that the people of Russia will do more than struggle toward a new beginning. They will struggle, yes, but their efforts will lead to far more than just a beginning. They will reach a crystallization point, when, after a long arduous process, conditions suddenly become right. One day, when students finally have enough books and lab equipment and computers; when people tire of reading Western trash and want to know what their own Russians are writing; when film makers finally have a budget to make a film; when English teachers no longer abandon their schools to take a job as secretary for a Westerner who can say only five words of Russian; when composers are no longer selling potatoes in the street; when parents have enough money to pay for piano lessons, dance lessons, skating lessons; when doctors have the equipment and pharmacies have the medications to provide genuine health care; when the air becomes breathable and the water becomes drinkable; when dancers can practice in a heated theater; when journalists are no longer shot on their doorsteps because of the articles they wrote; when veterans of the Great Patriotic War finally receive a pension they can live on; when teachers and doctors and factory workers and miners are finally paid a monthly salary on a regular basis; when men with machine guns no longer guard the door to the neighborhood bank; and, equally important, when the people of Russia realize that they were right all along: that poetry, and the magic of ballet, and the power and passion of a symphony, and the probing questions in a novel, and the incense and icons and reassuring words in their churches, are their foundation and their future.

Then, Russia will more than begin. Her people will blossom into the unexpected miracle of the next Renaissance.

A renaissance: a rebirth, a rethinking, a resuscitation of the human spirit. The next Renaissance will come from a people hungry to learn, to create, to explore, to build. And what they will build, above all, will not be the weapons of war, nor the trappings and trinkets of prosperity, but the concrete guarantees of peace.

This desperately needed Renaissance will come, with far greater likelihood, not from the frenzied electronic bustle of the Big Apple, nor from the blockbuster megabucks glitz of the Big Grapefruit, but from the poets and screenwriters and journalists of St. Petersburg, and of Poland, and of Hungary and Slovakia and Albania and what was once East Berlin: poets whose ink is black with the ashes of their parents' generation. The next Renaissance will come from the painters and composers, and from the economists and the ecologists of the City on the Neva, where the fledgling market economy will be embraced by a people who want not simply more, but better.

I would like to let Andrei, one of my students at the University, have the final word. In one of his essays, he wrote, "Don't believe all you hear about Russia is dying. We have big troubles, but when Peter the Great reformed old Russia, he suffered even more. After the first defeat in the war with Sweden, he said that it's just a lesson for the future. So today, we will learn our lesson from fighting with (economic) depression.

"There is an ancient Russian saying: 'Russians harness the horse slowly, but they ride fast.' So I'm inviting all Americans to Russia in 2026. I believe it will be paradise!"

No doubt about it: Andrei will work hard for the next thirty years.

Will we work together? Or will we continue to ignore America's historic opportunity?

Chapter Four

In 1991, the Soviet economy did not just collapse; it vanished. Factories throughout Russia had depended on components shipped from the various republics within the Soviet Union. When those republics broke away and became independent countries, they stopped shipping their axels and pistons and circuit boards into Russia, for they readily turned their attention toward trade with the West. The factories inside Russia, now without certain vital parts, could no longer produce their products, and thus their workers were idled.

During the 1980's, seventy percent of the workforce in St. Petersburg, a city of five million, had worked in military production, making everything from sonar for submarines to the nuclear missiles which were targeted on Washington. In 1991, the Cold War superpower disintegrated, and though its missiles remained targeted on Washington, the highly educated workers in this vast military-industrial complex were suddenly out of work. As a political and economic earthquake shattered their world, they found themselves out on the street, competing with thousands upon thousands of other skilled workers for jobs that did not exist.

During the Soviet period, the government had both subsidized the food industry, and had controlled prices. In 1991, both the subsidies and the control all but vanished. Prices rose quickly; or, in other words, the value of money diminished quickly. Life savings became worth 1/1000th of their original value; and the steady inflation did not stop until 5,000 roubles were needed to purchase what one rouble had purchased before. People began to barter, and to use that hideous capitalist currency of the Cold War enemy: the American dollar. Black market trade in dollars became the on-the-street economic system. People who had built the missiles aimed at Washington now used money with a picture of George Washington on the bills.

By 1995, inflation had slowed, and the government had decreed that only the rouble could be used in the Russian marketplace. But state workers such as teachers, doctors, and factory workers, miners and railroad workers, often went for months without a paycheck. The government simply did not have enough money to pay them. People kept working, hoping that one day they would be paid. Even idled workers showed up at their idled factories, with the hope that one day they would have a job, and a paycheck.

During the economic chaos of the early 1990's, a small portion of the population, many of them former Communist officials, made enormous sums of money by selling whatever they could get their hands on, from factory equipment and warehoused goods to military weaponry. They and their minions did not invest their wealth in their own country, but instead deposited billions upon billions of dollars in foreign banks, or invested the loot in foreign real estate. They became the New Russians, as wealthy as the old aristocracy under the tzar, while the vast majority of the Russian people were left with the wreckage and the rubble of their former country. The term "market economy" meant no more to most people than plunder on a national scale.

With Russian production at a virtual halt, business was reduced to the buying and selling of goods that had already been produced. The people of Russia were forced to offer a portion of their belongings in a desperation garage sale. Imports, at high prices, flooded the market, creating a chain of middlemen between the factories in Europe and America and the tiny Mom-and-Pop shops of Russia. Russian consumers could now purchase exotic Western goods, but that did not help their own industrial and agricultural production in the slightest.

Let us now visit the Russian marketplace, to see what all this meant for the average family in St. Petersburg.

PROGRESS IN THE MARKETPLACE?

In October, 1991, private enterprise was thriving in St. Petersburg. On the broad sidewalk in front of every Metro station, scores of people stood from dawn until midnight in every sort of weather, selling whatever they and their families were able to part with: books from the family library, potatoes from their country garden, shoes which the children had outgrown, a package of unused spark plugs, a pair of patched rubber boots.

A well-dressed man (who might have had a top-level engineering job a year ago,) displayed his wares on a small table: an assortment of copper pipes and valves, a few boxes of cigarettes, and five turnips. The woman beside him held up three dissimilar shoes: their mates were in the muddy plastic bag at her feet. Should you wish to try on one of her shoes, you would have to stand on one foot in a drizzle to do it.

Neither one of them tried to catch the attention of a potential customer. Cold and damp, they stared with weary eyes at the endless crowd sweeping past.

A young man sold potatoes out of the trunk of his car. An elderly man sold eggs to people who had brought their own empty cartons. A woman held a scarf of plastic over her head as she neatly arranged her radishes and onions on an upturned crate. She clutched the plastic more tightly at her neck, for the drizzle was turning to sleet.

Nearby, people stood in line to buy milk from the back of a truck with no name, no advertising. It was simply an old battered blue truck.

A fortunate few vendors sold their merchandise from kiosks: homemade wooden boxes eight feet by six, with a door cut into the back and a window cut into the front. Some of these booths were wired with electricity, though many were lit, (and heated through the winter,) by two candles flanking the window. Various members of the family worked in their kiosk from early morning to past midnight, while the Metro was open. They learned the fundamentals of this new thing called capitalism: how to find the goods that people wanted to buy, how to sell the goods without being robbed. They paid taxes, and learned how to pay as little as possible. They also paid the local mafia for "a roof", or protection. Some Russian entrepreneurs painted their wooden boxes with an attractive blue or green, and a few added a hand-painted sign. Their windows displayed an unpredictable variety of goods, and a customer had to search each window, kiosk after kiosk, until he found (perhaps) what he was looking for.

Horatio Alger, had he spoken Russian, would have felt right at home.

During my first visits to St. Petersburg, I would often teach at one school in the morning and at another school in the afternoon; hence I would have to search for a restaurant somewhere between them to have lunch. But the few scattered and very obscure cafes in 1991 offered little to eat. If Tanja and I could find a cafe, and if, once inside, we could find an unoccupied table, somebody else's dishes were on it, and were likely to stay on it. An alternating blend of Russian and American rock music blasted from a cassette player. The windows facing the street were taped shut against the winter draft, so we breathed not only the smoke of all the chain-smokers at the other tables, but the smoke of chain-smokers who had dined here six months ago.

No waitress appeared, so we walked over to the counter. Behind it were wall-to-wall liquor bottles and packages of cigarettes, and the door to the kitchen. A woman with a blank face stared at me. "Do you have a hot meal?" I asked in English. Tanja then translated into Russian. Since there was no menu, I suggested, "Chicken maybe, some potatoes, and a vegetable." The woman shrugged, turned her attention to the next customer, who ordered tea and a package of cigarettes.

Fifteen minutes later, fortified with nothing more than tea and sugar rolls, I hurried to another five hours of teaching. By late afternoon I was dizzy with hunger, and now a university student raised his hand and asked me to explain the American stock market.

Five years later, in 1996, people still stood outside the Metro selling potatoes and turnips. But the multitude of vendors now offered a broader variety of homegrown vegetables: parsley, carrots, apples, and melons from the independent republics in the south. In the autumn, people displayed freshly picked berries and mushrooms.

Much of the food on sale in 1996 was imported. On a frigid evening in January, a woman bundled in a fur coat stood behind two upturned crates. On one crate was a heap of frozen chicken legs. On the other crate were several bunches of bananas, imported from Central America. Both the chicken legs and the bananas were lightly covered with snow. The woman did not worry about keeping her drumsticks frozen. As for the bananas . . .

The enclosed kiosks were now more numerous, and they usually contained both electric lights and a small electric heater on the floor. Often the booths were capped with an illuminated MARLBORO sign. Some of the kiosks were metal trailers with wheels, which could be hauled from one market to another.

The marketplaces themselves were much more organized than they had been five years ago. Open stalls with a green canopy formed a neat rectangle near one Metro, with customers shopping along the outside, and vendors stomping their cold feet on the inside. Nearby, numbered kiosks with metal shutters stood in a row along the sidewalk. Both the stalls and the kiosks displayed an extensive variety of Russian and imported goods: shampoo from Norway, laundry detergent from a factory here in St. Petersburg, corn flakes from the ancient Russian city of Pskov, crackers from Stockholm. One stall offered the same brand of cat food that my grandmother in Utica pours into Oreo's bowl.

Flower vendors sell carnations, roses and cactuses throughout the winter. Their bouquets stand in homemade plexiglass boxes which are heated with candles to keep the flowers from freezing. On a snowy night, the red candle-lit roses are gorgeous exotic blossoms, protected in their boxes like tropical fish in a heated aquarium.

During the Soviet period, every item purchased in a government store had to be paid for individually, in advance. Customers pushed through the crowd to see what was available, and what it cost. Then they stood in line until they could pay the woman at a cash register and receive a receipt. They stood in line a second time until they reached the counter and could trade their receipt for a bar of soap. This process was repeated for a kilogram of carrots, a package of razor blades, a toothbrush. Calculations at the cash register were made on an abacus, an ancient Greek instrument with wooden beads which the merchant snapped back and forth with quick flicks of her fingers.

Now in 1996, private shops had proliferated and the lines had all but vanished. The ground floors of rundown buildings had been renovated into stores of every size and variety. Sometimes only one corner of a newly plastered room operated as a shop; the remainder of the room would be painted and filled with display counters as profits were ploughed back into the business. Though some proprietors still relied on the abacus, most clerks used hand calculators. If I failed to understand them when they told me the tally in Russian, they simply showed me the green digital number on their calculator.

Some shops still required a receipt for each item, but more and more enabled their customers to select goods from the shelves, then to pay for everything together at a check-out counter. The most modern supermarkets, usually joint-ventures with a foreign co-owner, were small by American standards, but they provided shopping baskets and sometimes even carts. The staff were generally helpful and polite, though prices were definitely higher than out in the street.

This outward appearance of progress, however, masked a critical flaw in the economic system. Yes, the neat rows of kiosks and the modern shops were well stocked in 1996. Capitalism seemed to have brought a degree of prosperity to the Russian people. But whereas most European and American stores offered a balanced blend of domestic and foreign goods, roughly sixty percent of the merchandise for sale in a Russian shop was imported. Thus, most of the money spent by each Russian household for food did not stay in Russia, but flowed in a vast fiscal river toward the West. Were Americans to import the bulk of their groceries from Canada and Mexico, our economy would be devastated and our food producers would be crippled. The situation would be all the worse during a major economic depression.

So it was in Russia: dairy products from nearby Finland, noodles from Iran, salt from Denmark and the Ukraine, tea from England, Kellogg's corn flakes from America. The Russian farmer, his collective no longer supported by the Soviet government, didn't have a chance.

On the individual level, the Russian people had responded to the economic crisis of the 1990's with unrelenting fortitude and hard work. They were doing their best to meet the Russian demand for high-quality products.

But on the national level, the economy had no solid foundation. The demand was domestic but the supply was predominantly foreign, and thus profits were not invested into local farms and industries.

In addition, high taxes crippled small businesses with limited capital. A group of businessmen in St. Petersburg stated in 1996 that taxes were "extortionate": they believed that government officials, often former Communists, did not want the business sector to become powerful, so they fed like parasites on the profits and thus preserved their bureaucratic positions of power and prestige.

The complex relationship between private enterprise and government regulation was further complicated by the role of the mafia, armed groups who operated on a local or national level, and who controlled vast amounts of money inside Russia. A true "market economy" responds to public supply and demand; Russia's economy during the 1990's, however, was artificially manipulated by mafia groups powerful enough to control nearly every level of trade, always to their own advantage.

During the years after the collapse of the Soviet Union, the Russian people, ordinary fathers and mothers, were building a new country virtually by themselves. They had no Roosevelt and his team of economic experts to lead them out of their Depression; they had no New Deal programs to provide work for the unemployed. They had no Marshall Plan, which jump-started the economies in Western Europe after World War II; no national program helped to get individual workers and farmers back on their feet. Instead, the Russian people struggled day after day to provide for their families, and thus they formulated their own version of Mom-and-Pop capitalism. American newspapers love to tell the tale of bumbling Russian governments, appalling corruption and collapsing banks, but rarely do we hear about the other ninety-five percent of the population, who build their small businesses and wait for the day when the pirates no longer have the upper hand.

Let's take a look at some 1996 figures.

A full-time professor at the University earned about $40 a month, if he was paid. At the current price for milk, $1.60 a gallon in October, 1996, and the comparably high price for other groceries, his monthly salary would enable him to feed his family for about a week. A meal at a small neighborhood restaurant cost about $5, so if a man took his wife out to dinner, he would spend a fourth of his paycheck. The St. Petersburg tradition of taking the children several times a year to see the treasures of their heritage—the ballet, the symphony, the great paintings in the museums, the performing bears at the circus—became increasingly difficult to afford. The annual summer vacation on the beach beside the Black Sea was replaced by work in the family vegetable garden, in order to have potatoes for the winter.

Most of the teachers I knew in St. Petersburg had two or three jobs. They taught their regular classes during the day, then taught commercial classes in Business English in the evening, and supplemented that income with private tutoring, or perhaps translation work, on weekends. That left little time for adequate preparation, or paper grading, or sleep.

A RUSSIAN ELECTION

Why on earth, you may ask, do the Communists do so well in Russian elections? Why, in December of 1995, did twenty-seven percent of the Russian voters elect Communist representatives for their Parliament? Baffled, Americans wonder why the party that enforced central planning, an economic policy that led to the virtual bankruptcy of the nation, should once again be given a major voice in the Russian government.

Faced with a choice of forty-three parties, and tired of economic reforms that seemed to be leading nowhere, many Russian voters yearned for the Good Old Days when the Soviet system guaranteed that every worker had a steady job and a paycheck, and a degree of dignity.

For many Russians, "democracy" meant empty campaign promises on television. They voted for "candidates" in a "democratic election", then they learned that the politician they had elected was embezzling funds and building a sumptuous summer house surrounded by armed guards. "Democracy" thus became just another deceptive slogan from the West.

The "market system" meant that a few thugs could make big bucks and drive a black Mercedes, while the majority of the people still lived in small cold apartments and could not afford a car. "Freedom of the press" meant that a journalist could write openly and truthfully about the injustices in Russian society, until someone blasted him with a machine gun on his doorstep. Democracy, the market system, and all the other innovations from the West had brought nothing but chaos. But when the Communists had been in power, people enjoyed stability, everyone had enough, and the streets were clean and safe.

The Russians were tired. I sometimes thought, looking into their faces, that they must be the most tired people on earth. They watched "Santa Barbara" on television, marveled at the elegant homes and huge cars, the dresses, the jewelry, the fast sex, and then they trudged to the market to buy a box of Italian noodles.

LOOKING FOR A CHRISTMAS TREE

Russians decorate spruce trees for New Year's Eve, and for their Christmas on January 6.

On the afternoon of December 31, 1995, I drove with my friend Dmitri around St. Petersburg in search of a tree for his family's apartment. Dmitri's old car, like most of the vehicles on the icy streets of the city, had summer tires; we skidded to a halt at intersections, then spun a wheel to get going again. My seat belt had a buckle, but the dusty belt itself was so slack that I would have been halfway through the windshield before it pulled tight across my waist. The feeble defroster might have done some good in October, but it didn't have a chance in December; Dmitri and I had to keep scraping the windshield if we were going to see anything through our frozen breath.

We drove to a half-dozen neighborhood marketplaces, and found everywhere in the city the same situation: a long line of people waiting in a cold dark courtyard for a truck that was rumored to be on its way with spruce trees. When it would arrive, no one knew. After hours of searching, we finally gave up and drove home. We had seen hundreds of people waiting in lines for a tree, in a city not far from the vast forests of northern Russia, yet we could not hang a single ornament. Where were the trucks? Sliding off snowy roads on their summer tires?

Dmitri told me that during the Soviet period as well, it had been difficult and sometimes impossible to find a tree. One year, rather than disappoint his little girl Ekaterina, he had to buy an artificial tree. Maybe we would have to get it out again this year, he said.

Ekaterina, now my colleague at the University, summed it up when Dmitri and I returned empty-handed to the apartment, "As we didn't have before, so we don't have now."

Undaunted, Dmitri tried again later in the evening. He returned with a spruce two feet tall which he had bought at a railroad station at the southern edge of the city. He explained that people could buy a license from the government which allowed them to cut up to three spruce trees somewhere outside the city, then to sell them at the station. If they sold more than three, they had to pay taxes, and a cut to the mafia.

We congratulated our hero, then I helped him to wind a string of colored lights around the tree. When we plugged them in, not a single bulb lit. I had heard about old-fashioned Christmas tree lights with series rather than parallel wiring, and now I knew that they still existed, in Russia. Together, systematically taking turns, Dmitri and I unscrewed and replaced each bulb, until suddenly our little spruce lit up with a splendid spiral of colored lights. Hurrah!

At midnight, we raised our glasses of vodka to toast the New Year. Ekaterina's family and I could hear the popping of fireworks outside the apartment windows: the city was celebrating. I wondered how long the people in those lines had waited, and whether the trucks had ever come. How does a father feel who returns with frozen feet to his apartment, where he must explain to his child that this year, they will have no tree?

For whom will he vote in the next election?

HER DAUGHTER'S ROSES

Rosie the Riveter has retired to St. Petersburg, Florida, where she spends her days picking up pink seashells on the beach, and playing shuffleboard. But here in St. Petersburg, Russia, women who once worked in the armaments factories during the war now stood outside in the rain and sleet and frozen mud while they tried to sell a handknit tablecloth, or packages of Camels, or frozen Snickers candy bars.

Walking to the Metro on my way to an evening class, I passed at least twenty women in their seventies who should have been home in their apartments, reading Pushkin to a grandchild. Instead they stood out in the weather for endless hours, risking pneumonia, offering odds and ends to the crowd swarming past them.

When I emerged from the Metro hours later, I recognized one of the grandmothers, for she had been here night after night, standing in the glow of a streetlamp. She had given at least fifty working years of her life to the Motherland, to Lenin, to her Soviet comrades, to their collective dream, and now she must give her remaining years to a "transitional market economy" that she cannot understand, and certainly does not believe in. What was the point of a Western free market, if the old people had to stand out in the snow?

I said good evening to her, "DOH-brih VYAY-chirh." With a cordial voice, she returned my greeting. I sounded like an American parrot miming a Russian guidebook, but she, her eyes brightening with a faint smile, spoke the words as Tolstoy would have spoken them.

I looked down at her battered apple crate, on which she displayed an oval slice of birch wood, about ten inches long and half an inch thick, with white bark forming a frame around it. The oval slice was painted with red and pink roses. I asked her if she had painted the roses. No, her daughter had painted them, she told me. She repeated with pride, to be sure that I understood: her daughter had painted the roses. I picked up the unique painting, already thinking of it as a gift for my grandmother. I held in my hands the work of a skilled artist who no doubt loved roses; I held in my hands a Russian treasure, offered on a cold night to a stranger. I asked the old woman bundled in a long gray coat—her eyes warm, her lips blue, her face wrinkled with the ravages of war, the years of deprivation, and the fading of her proletariat dream—how much she would like for her picture of roses.

She pulled off a thick brown mitten and held up four gnarled fingers. "Chih-TIH-ree dollar." Four dollars. By law, her price should have been in roubles, but she clearly wanted Western currency. I looked at her thin hand in the freezing air. Those fingers had fought Hitler. Those fingers had planted countless potatoes. Those fingers had once held a newborn daughter. Those fingers now hoped to hold foreign money, because her life savings were hardly enough to buy a week's groceries.

I gave her four wrinkled green singles, with an oval portrait of George Washington on each bill. Washington would have been proud of her spirit of free enterprise. But I think he would have preferred that she were home warming her feet in front of a Franklin stove.

She wrapped the hand-painted roses in a piece of tattered newspaper. Then she tried to tie the package with a bit of frayed twine, but her cold fingers could not manage the knot. I offered to help her; after some pointing and gesturing, she nodded that she understood, then she held the package while I tied the knot.

Why, I wondered, hadn't her people and my people started doing this a long time ago? What had been the point of all those nuclear missiles, and all those trillions of dollars and roubles? Why on earth can't we learn to say "Hello" in more than one language?

Isn't that what Peter the Great had wanted? When he was a young man, learning to build ships in the port of London in 1697, vessels were sailing from that very harbor to the New World. He almost certainly watched the white sails of a frigate as it glided down the Thames on its way to Boston or New York. Less than thirty years after Peter learned the trade of shipbuilding in London, young Ben Franklin arrived to develop his skills in the trade of printing. Surely Peter, who became the editor of the first Russian newspaper, would have enjoyed a pint of mead and a good long talk with the future author of *Poor Richard's Almanac.*

Two apprentice statesmen, determined to build a better world.

On May 16, 2003, the city that Peter founded will be 300 years old. Fireworks will no doubt light the sky over St. Petersburg, as they did in

Peter's time.

I can only hope that among my motivated students, a few states-men will emerge, a few brave leaders with dreams.

TODAY IN THE METRO

Deep in a dusty subway tunnel,
A woman my grandmother's age plays the violin
For people whose roubles are worth
Less and less each day.

Three meters from her stands another woman,
Not old, but ancient;
Her hair, wrapped in a green wool scarf,
Is not gray, but white.
Her eyes are too tired to watch
The endless crowd rushing, trudging, limping
Past her tiny outstretched hand.

I pause to listen to the violin,
For the song is perhaps an old Russian ballad.
One, two, three people stop briefly
To place coins (almost worthless) or paper money
In the tiny half-curled hand.
The great-grandmother does not look up,
But crosses herself as her lips speak a blessing.

Finally someone drops a bill into the violin case.

Today the musician plays for more than her own groceries.
A stranger old enough to be her mother
Reaches into the stream of a strange new Russia,
And so the violinist plays a song
Which the ancient woman no doubt knew
As a child,
And can sing in her heart.

Chapter Five

Let's take a look at the city itself, and what it was like to live there.

THE CITY ON THE NEVA

St. Louis is not merely a city, but a city on a river: it overlooks the broad, brown, slow-moving Mississippi. Manhattan is bounded by two rivers, the Hudson and the East; merging at the island's southern tip, they reach out through the Verrazano Narrows toward the rolling Atlantic. From her sandy beaches, Chicago scans the blue expanse of Lake Michigan, the first of several lakes that connect her with the world. San Francisco gazes from her hilltops at the golden sun spreading its afternoon sheen on the Pacific. Each of these cities is enrichened in her spirit by the waters that lap her shores.

So with St. Petersburg, for the Neva River runs right through the heart of the city. Here is a world capital where ocean-going ships dock in front of a neighborhood church. Where icebreakers are as much a part of urban life as trolley cars. Where seagulls are as common as pigeons.

When Peter became tzar of Russia in 1682 at the age of ten, his country was vast, but virtually landlocked. Russian tradesmen had no access to the Black Sea, for its shores were controlled by the Turks; Russia was thus unable to reach the markets of the Mediterranean. Nor was Russia able to trade by way of the Baltic Sea, for powerful Sweden controlled both the Neva River and the Gulf of Finland, which led out to the sea-kingdoms of the north.

After failing to breach the Turkish blockade to the south, Peter redirected his prodigious energies toward opening a route in the north. For twenty-one years, from 1700 to 1721, his inexperienced armies and newlycreated navy battled the professional forces of Sweden's king, Charles XII. Though defeated at Narva early in the war, Russia persevered, until decisive victories on both land and sea enabled Peter the Great to control the Neva, the Gulf, and the eastern shore of the Baltic Sea. The Russian fleet could now sail out to do business, or battle, with the world.

As soon as he had taken the Neva River from the Swedes, Peter began to build a fortress on an island near the river's delta, so that Russia's gateway to the sea could never be stolen from her. He thereby founded, in May of 1703, the future capital of his country. During the next eighteen years, while Peter commanded his ever-stronger armies and navy in battle after battle with Sweden, he also directed the planning and construction of a city which he hoped might one day rank among the great European capitals. He imported Italian architects to design his palaces and parks. He hired shipwrights from England and the Netherlands; with their help, he supervised first the construction of shipyards, and then the construction of ships. Being a man of many talents, he enjoyed taking up the shipwright's axe himself. He helped to build a number of homes for himself and his wife Catherine, all of them beside the water, so that when he was not aboard ship, he could at least look out at the swift flow of the Neva or the waves of the Gulf.

Today, Peter the Great is buried in a cathedral inside the walls of his fortress, on an island swept by the river. On the opposite shore of the Neva stands his equestrian statue in bronze: on a rearing horse, Peter stretches forth his arm and gazes upon the broad deep river that, nearly three hundred years later, still links his nation with the peoples of the world.

Dostoeyevsky walked along the Neva's granite embankment at night, his mind at work, probing the dark corners of the human soul.

Perhaps, while watching sunshine sparkle on the river, Tchaikovsky heard the opening bars of the dance of the Sugarplum Fairy.

Anchored at a fork in the river is the cruiser *Aurora*, the ship that fired, on the evening of November 7, 1917, the second shot heard 'round the world. Today the hundred-foot warship is a floating museum open to the public. People can stand on her metal deck and wrap a hand over the steel barrel of the six-inch gun that fired a blank at the Winter Palace; that shot signaled both the end of Kerensky's Provisional Government and the beginning of Lenin's Revolution. For upon hearing the night-shattering boom of that gun, armed workers and Bolshevik Red Guards entered the Winter Palace, rounded up the undefended ministers, and made themselves at home in what had once been the palace of the tzars.

While standing on the deck of the *Aurora* and staring out over the river, one can ponder three-quarters of a century of Soviet rule, and the wreckage it led to.

Further downstream, a handsome square-rigger is often docked beside the granite embankment. Its three tall masts, each with five spars, lit by the low September sun, form a grid of gold against the blue sky. I walked beside the sleek metal hull to the stern, where I read the vessel's name, *Mir*, which means Peace. Her home port is still written as "Leningrad". The *Mir* too is open to the public. Families trundle up the gangplank and explore her wooden decks. They cannot climb the rigging, but they can ascend a flight of steps to a platform from which they are able to look forward to the jutting prow, and upward into the webs of rope ladders. Aboard the *Mir*, the Russians can dream of a day in the past, and perhaps in the future too, when their country had a captain and a crew . . . and could spread its sails to the wind.

St. Petersburg was built where the river divides into four major branches and numerous smaller ones. The artery thus becomes four arterioles and a number of capillaries, nourishing the cells of the city. The people of St. Petersburg can stroll across 370 bridges, except in the middle of the night when the major bridges over the Neva are raised to let freighters and battleships pass through.

The people who live on the city's forty-two islands are naturally drawn to the water.

A woman seated on the granite wall of the embankment kisses her man, who stands with his arms wrapped around her. Oblivious to people passing by, they are granted a sanctuary aloof from the rest of us by the serene river behind them.

Nearby, a woman in a red coat leans against the wall and stares down at the river. Though she probably lives in a cramped apartment, surrounded by nondescript concrete buildings, the broad blue-gray sweep of the river provides her with all the space she needs to let her thoughts roam. The vast expanse of wind-rippled water is generous enough that all who wish, may float their dreams upon it.

Whenever I returned to my small cold room after a long walk beside the river, I made a cup of hot tea. The water for the tea came from the faucet, which drew from the municipal water system, which drew from the river. After having spent three days in bed as sick as a dying dog, the result of my drinking water straight from the tap, I bought a triple filter that connected to the faucet. The Russian and English instructions promised that this filter, manufactured in St. Petersburg, would remove "heavy metals, organic and inorganic matter, silt and sediment." After the water was filtered, I boiled it for several minutes in a pot on my hot plate, then I poured the water into my large Russian tea cup.

My students at the University frequently cited pollution in the river as one of their city's most serious problems. They asked if I could find books in English about the science of ecology. They wanted to learn how to clean up their river.

They wanted to make the Neva safe for drinking, for swimming, for fishing.

And they wanted its waters to be clean again because, as the river flows through their city, so it also flows through their souls.

AN AMERICAN IDEALIST IN THE CITY OF REALITY

In the autumn of 1995, I moved into an old Intourist Hotel, where I would live on the sixth floor in a tiny room while teaching at the University. I quickly made three discoveries. First, I learned that despite the chilly days and cold nights of September, in a city at the same latitude as southern Alaska, the building had no heat. Second, I learned that the hot water faucet in my bathroom sputtered damp air. The hot water that did not flow through the radiators was the same hot water that did not flow through the bathroom plumbing. Much in need of a shower after my long flight from New York, I asked the manager when the hotel would turn on the hot water.

He could not turn it on, he explained with a shrug. The city must turn it on. Most of the buildings in St. Petersburg were without heat.

"So," I asked, moving to the next obvious question, "when will the city turn on the hot water?"

Though I did not follow his entire dialectical explanation, I did catch two words which I recognized from my study of the Russian calendar: "October . . . or November."

"November!" Cold showers in an unheated bathroom until November!

He shrugged again, but assured me that the elevator would be operating soon.

I had already carried my heavy bags up six flights of stairs, and didn't give a darn anymore about the elevator.

My third discovery concerned the stove. Or rather, the lack of a stove. The hotel management had promised the University that the American professor would have cooking facilities, and the University had passed that promise on to me. The manager now politely informed me, as he would do for the next two weeks, (and off and on for the remainder of the year,) that the stove would appear 'tomorrow'. "ZAF-trah." That is a handy Russian word which means anything from sometime next week to early in the second decade of the next millennium.

After five days of increasingly greasy hair, (as I taught classes and attended faculty meetings,) I became desperate for a bath. In the dark and silent hours of late evening, I borrowed the samovar (an electric water heater for making tea) from the sixth floor lounge and heated a gallon of rusty cold water to a boil. I looked for a stopper so I could fill my bathroom sink with hot water. I found no stopper, so I stuffed a dirty sock down the drain. Then I poured delightfully steaming rusty water into the basin, and added enough cold rusty water from the faucet to bring my orange bath from boiling to good-and-hot. I dipped my Russian tea cup into the lovely, exquisite, civilized water, then managed to wash and (sort of) rinse my hair. Ahhhhhhhh! Perhaps I would survive after all.

But I still had no stove for cooking a proper dinner. I had managed with my rudimentary Russian to purchase a kilogram of potatoes from a vendor on the street. I had bought a block of butter. In the lounge cupboard I found odds and ends of plates and silverware, and even an old battered blue-and-white enamel pot that looked as if Krushchev's mother might have boiled potatoes in it.

But I had no stove! My belly was growling; my cheeks had become sunken; dark patches had appeared beneath my eyes. Thus, one week in Russia, and already I began to develop the instincts of a cunning peasant. Filling the samovar once again, I heated water to a boil, then dropped in six big potatoes. They sank down to the coils of the heating element. Twenty-five minutes later: perfect spuds!

The next morning, the kindly woman who supervised the sixth floor invited me to the lounge for a cup of tea. Maintaining a deadpan innocence, I watched as she sniffed the distinctly potatoey steam from her samovar. (I hadn't drained the water. With a long fork, I had speared the six potatoes, then devoured three of them.)

She frowned as she sipped her cup of tea. Sniffing the box of tea bags, she shook her head, baffled.

Though I did not understand everything she said, I did catch in her befuddled mutterings the world "kar-TOH-fel". Something about a 'potato'.

And so evolved our first cup of Earl Gray à la Potatoes. (Or perhaps, Potatoes à la Earl Gray, depending on one's dialectical viewpoint.)

A WINDOW ONTO CONTEMPORARY RUSSIA

My sixth floor windows were enormous, filling most of the wall. They looked down into a courtyard enclosed by an assortment of old concrete and brick buildings, most of them apartment buildings, one of them a school. The courtyard was a busy place during the day, and the apartment windows were lit at night, so that in a distant, urban way, I felt close to my neighbors.

Directly below my windows stood a row of maple trees in their full September blaze. Back home in the Adirondacks, I had always looked up at the orange and scarlet maples, vibrantly colorful against the crisp blue autumn sky; now I enjoyed looking *down* at their fluttering crowns. Across the courtyard stood a row of stately cottonwood trees, a lush wall of green tinged with September yellow. In earlier years, this courtyard may have been a park, an oasis of greenery undisturbed by the noise and traffic of the streets.

But now, most of the courtyard had been paved over and filled with parked cars, storage sheds, and a small odd-shaped soccer field enclosed by a rusty fence. Near the gate to the asphalt soccer field stood a battered, fire-blackened, overflowing garbage bin. Beside the bin was a heap of more garbage, growing larger by the day, for only rarely in 1995 was the nearly bankrupt city able to send out trucks to collect the trash. Anything that still had some potential value, such as broken furniture, old tires and scrap metal, was heaped in various corners of the courtyard. Thus below my window was a combination parking lot, playground and town dump.

Warming my hands around a morning cup of tea, I peered down and watched a mother walking with her small son as she escorted him to school; they walked across black asphalt speckled with yellow leaves. Babushkas wearing red and green scarves swept the ground around their doorways with brooms made of twigs, then they set out food for the stray cats. Businessmen with briefcases hurried to their offices. Loiterers without briefcases leaned against a brick wall and smoked a cigarette.

On Sunday afternoon, shouting boys played soccer in their trapezoidal court. One goal was a pair of soggy cardboard boxes taken from the garbage heap; the other goal was a truck tire that stood upright, and a lump of concrete.

Nestled between the crimson maples and yellow-green cottonwoods was an auto repair shop where trucks from Brezhnev's time roared and rumbled, venting clouds of black smoke that drifted across the courtyard, while men smoking cigarettes leaned over the engines and tinkered with a carburetor. VROOM! VROOOM! VROOOOM!, right behind the school. This shop operated from eight in the morning until eight at night, though its hours were often extended.

The auto repair shop also installed car alarms. At least once an hour throughout the day, an alarm suddenly filled the courtyard with its cadence of electronic screams and wails, buzzers and beepers and sonic blasters, sounding much as a robot would sound if it were kicked repeatedly in the groin.

The shop had a marvelous policy of customer satisfaction: after each new alarm was installed, the proud owner was invited not only to test his new purchase, but to play it through its cadence two or three times until he became familiar with its particular sequence of soul-shattering screams. This process was extremely important, because once familiar with his own personal car alarm, the owner, when awakened in the middle of the night, could know whether it was his car or somebody else's that was being broken into. During the two-minute, three-minute, five-minute acoustic demonstration, every apartment building around the courtyard gritted its concrete teeth and stood on brick tiptoes . . . until the customer, satisfied that his car was now secure, pushed a tiny button to turn off his alarm, paid his roubles, and drove away.

At night, snuggled in my Norwegian sleeping bag with the old-fashioned windows swung wide open, I could hear maple leaves rustling whenever a breeze managed to sweep down into the courtyard.

I could hear as well the deep sustained voice of a ship's horn, calling over the rooftops: a farewell from a freighter sailing out the Neva River into the Gulf of Finland.

Sometimes the quiet outside was riven by the shrill lament of a tomcat, whose feelings I well understood, for while I lived in St. Petersburg, I fell in love at least twice a day.

Best of all, the chimes of Saint Nicholas Cathedral rang out every fifteen minutes with their faint tinkling melody. And on the hour, an enormous bell tolled with indisputable certainty that the time was now one, two, three, four, five o'clock in the morning.

Then suddenly I was jarred bolt upright in my sleeping bag, my heart thumping with terror, because a cosmic blaster aimed through the window at my body by some alien space ship was shattering me into sonic-shocked atoms!

But no, it was just another car alarm down in the courtyard, wailing and buzzing and mega-burping in the middle of the night, waking up at least a thousand people. Why, I wondered, was the damn thing shrieking? (And I wondered too if anybody else wondered.) A short in the wiring? Or was somebody, three, four, five times a night, really stealing a car?

I could have staggered out of bed and peered down through the maples. Or I could wait with my fingers in my ears . . . . and wait . . . and wait, until after several frenzied minutes, some tiny digital switch finally signaled OFF. . . . and the courtyard savored the balm of silence.

Before I fell asleep again, I heard the faint cathedral chimes ringing their reassurance and their benison, as they had done through all the years of Communism. As they had done in the time of the tzars.

Such were the sounds of a country struggling, for the first time in its thousand year history, toward the blessings of freedom in the modern world.

A LACK-OF-PROGRESS REPORT

You know you're in trouble the moment you buy a box of corn flakes. On one side of the box, you read CORN FLAKES in English. On the other side of this package from Pskov, you read two words in Russian, each about seventeen syllables long, the second word ending with a backwards R.

My Russian teacher is a very nice woman who deserves better than a Bear of Very Little Brain for a student. But in my own defense, I have discovered that Russian is not a language; it's a code. Consider, that first there is the printed Cyrillic alphabet, which Saint Cyril created in the ninth century so the Slavic people could read the Bible. He borrowed heavily from the Greek alphabet, then he added some inventions of his own. As a result, a B is really a V, an H is an N, a P is an R, and X is pronounced like an H when you have terminal tertiary tonsillitis. A small b can represent any number of sounds ranging from an actual B to, if the b is followed by an undotted i, an ee that is not really an ee but a brief glottal wheeze.

Consider further, that the handwritten Russian alphabet *differs* from the printed Russian alphabet, so that a printed Delta (for D) becomes a small handwritten g. Now why, you wonder, should a D become a g? For the same reason that a printed T becomes a handwritten m. But not just an ordinary m: it may be an upside down m, depending on the loopy script of the writer. The letter I becomes a handwritten n, which may/must (I am still uncertain on this point) be written upside down, resembling exactly the handwritten H, which is really an N. String together eight or ten horseshoes and you have a Russian word of eight or ten different letters and an unknown number of syllables. String together a dozen such words on the blackboard and you have mmmmmmm mmmmmmmmmmmm mmmm mmmmmmmmmm mmmmmmmmmmmmmmmmm, which written upside down becomes uuuuuu uuuuuuuuuu uuuu uuuuuuuuuu uuuuuuuuuuu, (with the cursive letters pressed more closely together,) which my teacher does not allow me to translate, for I am forbidden to speak a word of English.

This Russian code is not done with me yet, for it has a third, (and top secret,) variation. Vowels are really a camouflage, for rarely are they pronounced as they appear. O's become ah's, ya's become ee's, ee's aren't really ee's at all because they have a double dot over them, and so they become yoh's, except that the Russians often omit these double dots, because they all know that they are there. So yeeyee is actually yohyoh, just like the yoyo you had when you were a kid.

Consonants change too, so that the one-armed gallows that you finally figure out is a G, is not always pronounced like a G, but like a V, though only in some cases, such as when it's raining outside on a Tuesday, or the stoplight is just turning yellow, or your left foot is cold.

Nor is a word simply a word, but rather the protean root of a whole batch of look-alikes with different endings, depending on whether the plural possessive is masculine, feminine, or neuter, and depending as well on whether it's April or October when you happen to use that particular noun, and depending further, (in the case of an adverbial phrase inside of a dangling participial clause, either subordinate or insubordinate,) on whether or not you are wearing blue socks, black, gray, or brown, all of which may or may not indicate a different ending. In fact, students of Russian are advised to study the language in pairs, so that one student can concentrate on the root words, while the other student concentrates on the endings; together in conversation, they should do fairly well.

Even people's names have different endings. Ekaterina becomes Katya, and then, on more familiar terms, Katushka. Natalia becomes Natasha, Dmitri becomes Dima, Tatiana becomes Tanja, Mikhail becomes Misha, Pavel becomes Pasha, and Alexander becomes, for reasons unknown to my Western mind, Sasha. So if you're tired of being Bob, plain old Bob, go to Russia. They'll fancy you up with a whole panoply of suffixes.

Further, dear reader, in addition, and moreover, not only can the multitude of devious, divers and elusive endings change, but internal vowels may change as well. In fact, a vowel, without any warning, may abruptly disappear, leaving a cluster of consonants jumbled together without a glimmer of breathing space between them.

(Every once in a while the student tried to disappear too, but my teacher kept her snarling, underfed Russian wolfhound on guard at the classroom door.)

All this, and we still haven't gotten any further than the Testing-Your-Knowledge quiz at the end of Chapter One in my four-inch-thick book of Basic Russian Grammar.

Various forms of gruesome and hideous tortures have been carried out in the dark damp dungeon of the Peter and Paul Fortress. Peter the Great ordered his son Alexis to be slowly brutalized to death in one of those stone-walled cells. My Russian teacher and I now re-enact that historical scene, I as the battered and bloody Alexis, she as the grim and merciless Peter. She is particularly adept at speaking Rapid Russian, without a pause for commas or periods, able to enunciate one thousand eight hundred and ninety-six Slavic words in just under thirty seconds, ending always with the upturned tone of a question . . . . which I am supposed to answer. While I search my scrawled and scribbled notes for some clue, she jabs one of her branding irons deeper into the hot coals. Already my body is covered with raised red welts of backward R's that are Yah's instead of Yoh's, and B's which I forgot are really V's. And many are the stripes of the lash when I remembered the future perfect most imperfectly.

Now I know why Lenin moved to Switzerland, and why Trotsky lived in New York. The former needed to hear a Tyrolean yodel, and the latter craved a healthy dose of Brooklynese, in order to get a grip on their vowels.

nota bene: Cyril had a lot of extra b's in his typesetter's box of letters. He sprinkled them into the spelling of many Russian words, so as not to waste them, sometimes injecting a 'b' into the middle of a word, sometimes tacking it on at the end. (These are little b's, not capital B's, which are really V's, or v's if the B is inside a word, although it still remains a capital B. See?) A 'b' placed somewhere inside a word may represent a 'soft sign' or a 'hard sign', indicating two different pronunciations; these two b's differ only in a tiny flag to the left at the top of the stem of the hard b, and the lack of a flag at the top of the stem of the soft b, (not to be confused with another b without a flag, which is followed by an undotted i and accordingly sounds a bit like the ee before the noose draws tight and the neck snaps,) also not to be confused with a 'b' with a slightly larger flag to the *right* at the top of its stem, indicating that this 'b' really is a 'b', and, believe it or not, should be pronounced like a 'b', as in 'Bother,' said Pooh.

Although grammatical explanations vary from book to book, *one* of my Concise Pronunciation Guides reveals that a 'hard b' indicates "mute": thus, no sound at all.

It was the first Russian letter which I mastered, and it will always remain my favorite.

(to be continued, unfortunately)

Chapter Six

To understand the people of St. Petersburg, an American visitor, whether here as a tourist or on business, must learn about the Nazi siege that battered this city with a cruelty that no American city has ever had to endure. Your conversations with Russians will be severely limited, and you will be viewed as naive, even childish, unless you understand the war that took several members from virtually every family.

THE 900-DAY SIEGE OF LENINGRAD

Inside the Museum of the History of St. Petersburg, (Rumiantsev Palace, 44 English Embankment,) we see a replica of a piece of bread, about the size of a third of a banana: the daily ration for two and a half years, while the German army gripped the city of Leningrad in a stranglehold. From June of 1941 until January of 1944, the city starved, the city froze, the city endured bombs and artillery shells falling anywhere and at any time . . . and the city refused to surrender to the surrounding Nazi troops. That bit of bread, and a bucket of water drawn from the river, kept them going through three northern winters. People who appeared well-fed during the siege, their faces pink, their eyes bright, were suspected of being cannibals. The frozen bodies heaped at the gates of cemeteries often had chunks of meat cut out of them. No one asked in the markets whether the meat patties on sale contained horse meat, dog meat, or otherwise.

At the Museum, we see another exhibit: a child's wooden sled with two old-fashioned tea kettles and a water pitcher on it. The sled was pulled to a hole in the ice on the Neva, where, unprotected by buildings, people with frostbitten fingers hoped to fill the teapot with water before an artillery shell hit them. Around the holes in the ice were rings of corpses, frozen until the river thawed in April.

An oil painting shows another use for a child's sled: though small, it could be used to transport a body. Out on the ice of the river, with Peter the Great's fortress and cathedral in the misty background, a young woman has collapsed into the snow beside the sled, her face filled with exhaustion and despair. Will she find the strength to pull the adult body on the sled the rest of the way to a cemetery? Or will she simply lie down beside her father, and silently join him?

We pause in front of a photograph of Tanya Savicheva, an eleven-year-old girl who kept a diary in her small notebook: each page, affixed to the wall beneath her picture, records the death of a member of her family during the first winter of the war. Every Leningrader knows about Tanya, and they know too that she herself died while she and other children were being evacuated from the city.

Tanya would have been sixty-eight years old today.

A CEMETERY AS LARGE AS AN AIRPORT

From the Museum, we take the Metro and then a bus to Piskaryovskoye Memorial Cemetery, north of the city, where we confront mankind's recent past.

Two small stone buildings flanking the cemetery entrance contain an exhibit of photographs taken during the Great Patriotic War. The first picture, taken on June 22, 1941, the day that German planes and tanks thundered across the border into the Soviet Union, shows a frantic mother holding the hands of her two children as she runs with them across a field of mud. Behind them are other women, other small children, who flee from the bombs that have destroyed their village.

Stepping to another photograph, we stare at a boy who wears bandages wrapped around his head. With wide-open eyes that witness, the boy stares back at us.

We stand before a portrait of a man with a sunken face, his cheeks deeply hollow, as if he had lost forty pounds in the last few months. In his hand he holds a chunk of bread, as precious as anything his fingers have ever gripped.

Near the end of this photography exhibit, we stand once again in front of a picture of Tanya. Like many Russian schoolgirls, she had a bow in her hair. The Russians visiting the cemetery today lean forward and read replicas of the nine pages from her notebook.

On the ledge above Tanya's picture, someone has placed two fresh red and white carnations.

We now walk through a gate between the two museums, and enter the vast cemetery, its grass and birch trees lightly dusted with the winter's first snow. Directly in front of us burns an eternal flame, perhaps a foot tall, framed by a square of black marble. We pause to stare at the flame, flickering and dancing in a place that is otherwise very still.

A Russian family stands beside us. A girl with a white bow in her hair holds a bouquet of pink carnations. At a word from her mother, she takes one flower from her armful and places it on the black marble near the silent orange flame. Other flowers have already been laid here by earlier visitors, earlier pilgrims.

Looking beyond the flame, we see a set of steps leading down to a broad gravel path, about two hundred meters long. At the far end of the path we see a tall statue of a woman, holding out her arms to the vast rippled lawn in front of her.

As we walk along the frozen path, we see that the immense lawn on both sides is divided into long, narrow, elevated rectangular plots that ripple at right angles to the path: these are the grass-capped trenches, each a mass grave. Near the end of each long mound, facing the path, is a granite marker; on these markers are inscribed no names, but simply the year during which thousands of corpses were buried in that particular trench. We walk past a stone engraved with 1942, then past another 1942, and another 1942. The snow-dusted mounds behind these markers stretch at least the length of a football field. Flowers have been laid on nearly every marker: white daisies, yellow jonquils, and roses whose red and pink and white buds will never open, but are doomed to freeze here.

We walk, we walk, we walk, past 1943, past 1943, past 1943, looking left and right at graves that seem to reach in both directions almost to the horizon. 1944, 1944, 1944, 1944. Nowhere in America do we have a cemetery like this. Even in our stately Arlington, with its neat rows of stones, we could not stand in the presence of so many stolen lives, so many devastated dreams.

1945. 1945. 1945.

The girl with the white bow in her hair places another pink carnation on a gray, snow-flecked stone: a flower for someone she never knew, whose photograph is perhaps at home on the living room wall.

At the end of the path which virtually every person in this city has walked, the girl and her father help her limping grandmother to climb a broad set of steps. Following them, we too stand before the tall weather-darkened bronze sculpture of the Motherland. With stern dignity in her face, she looks upon the expanse of land where her children lie. In her outstretched hands she holds a garland, as if she would lay it upon their graves. She is as much a part of the spirit of St. Petersburg as the Statue of Liberty with her torch is part of New York, or as the solemn Abraham Lincoln in his Memorial is part of Washington. She is not an armored warrior calling her countrymen to arms and military glory; she is not a muscled peasant defending Marxist-Leninist ideologies. She is a woman, her heart both laden with grief and brimming with compassion.

Behind her stands a wall with relief sculptures, and a long inscription in Russian. We listen to the girl's somber voice as she reads the memorial to her grandmother, who nods silently at the truth of this testament to the tragedy and heroism of the people of Leningrad.

The girl with flakes of snow on her coat does not read in a book about the history of her country. Speaking clearly for her grandmother, she reads aloud the history of her own family. She will not close a book on a bookmark; she will place her pink carnations, one by one, on the cold sacred stones.

The snowflakes are growing thicker while we walk back along the path; we zip up our coats. As we approach the steps that lead up to that silent, determined flame, we encounter a wedding party which has just arrived at the cemetery. The groom wears a handsome dark suit, the bride wears her beautiful white gown; both carry a bouquet of red roses. By tradition, they have come here after the wedding service, and before the festivities at the reception, to place their roses on the black marble at the foot of the Motherland.

In the happiness of today and the plans for tomorrow, the suffering and the strength of yesterday are not forgotten. Those who could not attend the wedding, those whose sacrifice made this wedding day possible, are remembered by a young man and a young woman whose first act as a married couple is to walk the long, long path together with their bouquets of red roses.

THREE PIETAS

At the southern edge of St. Petersburg, where the Russians stopped

the German battering ram with an impregnable human wall, we visit
Victory Square. Unlike the cemetery, Victory Square is not a quiet
place behind a fence; it is in the middle of a multi-lane traffic circle on
the main highway into the city. Nearly everyone who arrives at
Pulkovo Airport and then drives into St. Petersburg passes the towering
obelisk and the three groups of statues in front of it.

High on the granite obelisk are dates written in gold: 1941-1945.
At its base, a tall bronze worker holding a hammer and a tall bronze
soldier holding a machine gun stand shoulder to shoulder, staring south
with unrelenting watchfulness and stern determination. The enemy
shall not pass.

In front of these two guardians, to the left and right atop long
pedestals, two rows of bronze figures represent the people of wartime
Leningrad. A young woman holds a folded stretcher. A mother says
farewell to her son, who is slightly taller than she is. Two women in
kerchiefs pour molten metal into molds to make artillery shells. Four
soldiers advance toward the front, rifles and a flag in their hands; their
frozen energy reminds me of the dynamism in the American sculpture
of the Marines raising their flag at Iwo Jima. Two women scan the sky,
searching for enemy planes. A soldier wraps his protective arm around
a young girl.

These figures, raised above the traffic circle and thus silhouetted
against the sky, are both defiant and vulnerable. They are heroes, but
human heroes, who a short time ago were leading quiet civilian lives.
Veterans driving past are able to say to themselves, or to their grandchildren, "Yes, that was us."

Behind the obelisk is a ring of stone with a gap in it: the gap repre-
sents the breaking of the blockade. In the center of this circular wall of
stone, sunken below the traffic and so removed from the bustle of daily
life, three pairs of bronze figures take us back to the agony of a city under siege. Each pair is a realistic pieta: a woman holds her dead child; a
woman supports another woman who is perhaps not quite dead; a
young soldier supports a staggering grandmother.

These three pietas, unveiled on the 9th of May, 1975, the 30th anniversary of the Soviet victory over the Nazi invader, do not depict the
Virgin Mary holding the body of Jesus. The figures are not divine. The
Leningrad pietas depict people, in a way which clearly states that
human life is sacred.

AT HOME WITH TWO SURVIVORS

One Sunday evening, Tanya and I visited her grandmother, Lybov, and her great-aunt, Klavdia. The two elderly sisters lived together in a drab concrete apartment building that resembled the hundreds of other drab concrete apartment buildings crowded like upright dominoes around the periphery of the city. We entered through a back door, for the building's front door was mysteriously locked. The lobby was dark; the light bulbs had either burnt out, or someone had stolen them. Tanya found the elevator, which opened with a breath of stale cigarette smoke. We stepped into the tiny box, rumbled upward, then stepped out into a dark corridor. Tanya led the way, then knocked on a steel door. When it opened, pouring light into the hallway, we were greeted by two smiling matriarchs, Klavdia and Lybov. The fragrance of freshly baked cakes washed over us like a domestic benison. Tanya and I entered an apartment packed with the books, photographs and elegant furniture of several generations.

The white-haired sisters ushered us into a combination living room/dining room, where we beheld a table splendidly set with a white tablecloth, the household's best china, and a half-dozen varieties of homemade cakes. As we made our way through this confectionery feast, washed down with hot tea, I glanced at Lybov, sitting in a black dress across the corner of the table from me. Her blue eyes, filled with curiosity and ready humor, were watching me. The moment my plate was half-empty, she would offer me something more. Tanya proudly informed me that the sisters had been baking for two days in preparation for our visit.

Lybov had been born in 1910, when the tzar Nicholas II ruled Russia from his residence, the Winter Palace, only a short walk from her girlhood home. She was four when war broke out with Germany; Nicholas changed the name of the city from its original Germanic form, Sankt Peterburg, to the Russian version, Petrograd. She was seven when the tzar abdicated, and still seven when, nine months later, the Bolsheviks filled the tzar's palace with their proletariat troops. Lybov was eight, nine, ten during the Civil War, and fourteen when Lenin died in Moscow; the name of her city was changed to Leningrad. She was a teenager when Stalin gained control of the government, and a young woman in her twenties during the Terror. She became a mother in 1940, and a year later found herself with an infant daughter trapped in a city at war.

She and her child and her sister Klavdia were sitting together in their kitchen when a German bomb crashed through the roof of their apartment building . . . and did not explode. The child thus survived to become Tanya's mother.

Lybov was a dedicated worker during the years of reconstruction after the war. As the Cold War progressed, she lived in a city that became a first-strike nuclear target. Recently, she witnessed the unraveling of the Soviet Union, of the national economy, of everything she had worked for. In 1991, as statues of Lenin toppled, the name of her city once again became Sankt Peterburg. Her life had coincided with the violent beginning, the brutal consolidation, the heroic defense, the prolonged stagnation, and the rapid disintegration of Communism.

An old black cat curled up on a chair beside me, oblivious to the festivities, for the cat, Tanya told me, was deaf. Lucky cat, I thought, to live out your years here in this snug apartment. In 1942, Lybov and Klavdia would have eaten you.

"More cake?" asked Lybov, offering me a fourth piece. "What, you aren't hungry?"

When I was so full of sugar-sprinkled cakes and gingerbread cookies and homemade cranberry jam that I could not eat another crumb, I sat back in my chair with a silent groan. "Spah-SEE-bah bol-SHOY," I said to my two hostesses. A *big* thank you.

Now it was Klavdia's turn to look after the American guest. She handed me an old leather-bound album of photographs. "John, you can meet our family."

Turning the fragile pages slowly, I examined brown-tinted portraits of men and women in their best suits and dresses; they stood stiffly in a studio, and they stood almost as stiffly on a front porch. I looked closely at a snapshot of a young woman working in her garden. Of a man rowing a boat. A bearded soldier in uniform.

I recalled the old photos of my own family, taken in upstate New York and now collected in an equally fragile old album. We had often laughed at the brown-tinted portraits of well-dressed people standing stiffly in a studio. And we had howled at snapshots of chubby women and a beanpole man, grinning together in their bathing suits at Sylvan Beach. One old classic was a picture of my mother as a girl, sitting with her whole family around a summertime picnic table. I remembered, too, a photo of Mom's father's mother (a stern tyrant) wearing a sun bonnet as she worked in her grape arbor. And a photo of Dad's father (always jovial) smoking his cigar while he floated in a rowboat.

And there was a photo of my mother's brother, just a teenager in his white Navy uniform, home on leave before he shipped out as a tail gunner aboard an aircraft carrier in the Pacific. He came home in 1945. Yes, he came home.

I wished I had that old album now, so I could show Lybov and Klavdia pictures of my family in America.

I wanted to show them a sampling of American people, whose lives had also been shattered by Hitler. People whose lives had been directly threatened by Stalin, when he ordered, secretly, and then openly, the construction of an arsenal of nuclear weapons. People who had been threatened by Krushchev, who banged his shoe on the desk at the United Nations and promised to bury us. People who had been threatened by Brezhnev, who ordered Soviet troops into Afghanistan, and thereby ignited another front in the Cold War.

Drinking my cup of strong Russian tea, (which I knew would keep me awake for half the night,) I turned page after page of Russian faces looking out at me: people who ate cabbage instead of corn, who made beet soup instead of pea soup, who wore funny old-fashioned flat caps, and ribbons in their hair.

Allies during the Great Patriotic War, adversaries during the following four decades, our two nations have long regarded each other with profound suspicion.

What can we learn from each other? Very little, until we learn to work together. Then our mutual education will finally begin.

Sitting with Klavdia's album in my lap, I remembered the night when my father gave me my first pair of binoculars. We went out to the backyard that evening and looked at the moon. He showed me how to focus one eyepiece, and then the other eyepiece, so that the ivory-white ball with its overlapping craters became surprisingly sharp and three-dimensional.

Since that evening, the Russians have circled the moon with their rockets, and the Americans have walked on it. Were our two countries ever able to focus our separate eyepieces on a shared future, we would discover that we had much to learn from each other, and that we both, together, had an extraordinary journey ahead of us.

A RUSSIAN PRAYER

Reach deep inside me, please, and find my heart.
Take away a century of woe,
Tell the ghosts of war and strife to go,
And make the gods of weaponry depart.

Reach deep inside me, please, and find my soul.
Take away the curse of clinging fear,
Let unrelenting doubt no more appear,
Slay divisive anger, and make me whole.

Reach deep inside me, please, and find a man
Whose heart has room enough for all the love
The world deserves, and then will He above
Grant my soul the means to understand.

Help me please to clean away the dross;
So shall a life renewed replace the loss.

Chapter Seven

Yes, it was cold in my tiny apartment, 53° through most of the winter; and yes, it was even colder in the classroom, 46° through most of the winter. Even in apartments that were fairly warm, the concrete-slab floors were like the floors of walk-in freezers.

But outside! Let's take a walk in the magical realm of a Russian winter.

WINTER IN ST. PETERSBURG

I have lived in the Great North Woods of the New York Adirondacks when the cold coming down the stovepipe was so fierce, the flames froze in my stove; I have lived with the reindeer people on the rolling, snow-covered tundra of northern Norway, where people speak of the temperature as 40°, not bothering to say they mean *minus* 40°; and I have lived on the Norwegian coast above the arctic circle, where codfish fresh from the sea were so cold that our hands ached while we cleaned them.

But I have never seen the wintry air sparkle in the sunshine as it does in St. Petersburg. Those are not flakes of snow glinting in the sunlight, nor is it a mist that catches the light with a suffused glow. The moisture in the air of this seaport has frozen into tiny bits of ice that glitter by the jillions. The sparkles are not falling like snow; they are part of the air itself, and as I walk to work on a frigid morning, I love to look up at a fine dust of diamonds twinkling against a blue sky.

The enormous oak trees in the park appear at first to be covered with snow. But no, their black branches are clad with soft delicate white crystals of frost. The moist, gently drifting air from the nearby Gulf of Finland has garnished every twig with a powdery rime. The uppermost boughs form a canopy of lace.

On the ground, heavily bundled people shuffle along snowy paths on their way to work; above us is a forest of white where sparkling fairies play.

I love to run a few kilometers every evening along the embankments of the frozen Fontanka River. The full moon shines over the rooftops of aristocratic palaces and proletarian factories facing the river, their facades a dark backdrop to the long white stripe of ice. The sidewalk along the embankment is covered with packed, squeaky-cold snow that provides a perfect footing. As I cruise at a steady pace, puffing plumes of moonlit air, I watch a variety of dogs bounding across the frozen river while their owners walk with a leash coiled in their hand. The jubilant hounds gallop as fast as their apartment-atrophied legs will carry them; then they turn on skidding paws, and race back to the man who was kind enough to give them a half-hour of freedom.

The kids have cleared a rectangle on the ice where they play hockey, sort of. The goals are defined by a pair of something at each end, though that something changes almost every night: it may be boards, boxes, twisted metal, or a broken chair. Some of the kids have actual hockey sticks; most use a scrap of wood. Stone steps lead down from the embankment to the river; the boys have no bench, so they sit on the bottom step when they put on their skates. The steps and surrounding ice are littered with beer cans, cigarette butts and even household trash. While these kids learn to work a hockey puck, they also learn to ignore the trash, for it will all wash away when the ice melts in the spring.

Thus are my evenings runs a blend of wintry exultation and post-Soviet gloom.

And then, as happens so often while I stumble through the ruins of modern Russia, I meet someone who towers above the rubble.

I was out taking pictures of the kids in a park one snowy afternoon. Some of my pals had sleds and some had skis, but most were sliding in their boots down a narrow stripe of ice. Like Russian surfers with their feet spread and their arms outstretched, they zoomed with a laugh past my clicking camera.

Later, I took pictures of skaters on a frozen pond. Two grandparents held a wobbly toddler between them, lifting him by his arms so he could scuffle forward on his blades. A girl in a red dress skated backward over the rough ice with surprising grace; her friends called to her, but she paid no attention to them as she concentrated on her form.

Eventually I wandered over to a hockey rink, a real rink with a wooden wall around it and proper goals, or at least the frames of goals, for they had no nets. Young boys practiced at one end, older boys at the other. A man skated back and forth between the two groups, calling out to various youngsters as they passed the puck and took their shots.

I was trying to take pictures (it was exceedingly difficult to focus in subdued winter lighting on players zipping and looping around the ice) when the coach skated over to me. I was afraid he might object to my intrusion with a camera and ask me to stop. Instead, he said hello and offered to shake hands. Pleased that an American would want to photograph his boys, he called them over for a group portrait. The kids quickly assembled, the younger in front, the taller in back. I focused on faces that ranged from boisterous exuberance to reserved curiosity. The coach's expression of pride lasted through all three shots.

Now whenever I have a free afternoon, I return to the hockey rink. I am always welcomed with a handshake from Vladimir. Once he invited me into the nearby locker room, where I found an abundance of benches and lockers in good repair. On the walls were photos of earlier hockey heroes. Vladimir's desk was a paragon of order: his carefully arranged papers flanked four neatly stacked hockey pucks. He pointed to a row of trophies atop a cupboard: he had coached winning teams of hockey during the winter, and of soccer during the summer. Several boys appeared at his office door while we talked. A quick question, a quick answer from the coach, and the boy was off to the rink.

Here, I thought with a teacher's grateful heart, is one of the keys to Russia's future. A caring adult, a bunch of eager kids, and (somehow) enough financial support to maintain a real hockey rink.

Never mind that now as I type these pages in my ice box of an apartment that I wear wool underwear from Norway, a wool cap from Iceland, and three layers of flannel Adirondack shirts. Never mind that my nose is red and my fingers are blue.

I hope the winter is a long one, so the ice on Vladimir's hockey rink will last until April.

A WEEKEND ON SKIS

In February of 1996, Tanja and her son Pavel invited me to spend a weekend at a ski lodge on the shore of the Gulf of Finland, northwest of St. Petersburg. Carrying bags and backpacks filled with winter clothing, we first rode on the stuffy Metro, then on an overheated train, and finally on an unheated bus with frost on the windows and frozen puddles on the floor. We walked the final leg of our journey, carrying our luggage for about a kilometer along a snowy lane through a spruce forest. The deep fluffy powder on the boughs of the trees, the late afternoon sun tinging the drifts with gold, and especially the scent of spruce in the cold air, were all a balm to my weary soul. After five months of filthy air in St. Petersburg, where most of the old cars and trucks still burned leaded gas and a lot of oil, I had journeyed to a wintry paradise where I could inhale deep breaths of cold, clean, forest-scented air.

We passed through the gate of a Pioneer Camp, a seaside camp for children during the summer, a ski lodge for families during the winter. The buildings of this once-Soviet camp were brick boxes with all the charm of a crumbling flophouse in the Bronx. When we entered our four-story "lodge", I noted that jagged chunks of concrete were breaking loose from the floors, the steps, the walls. Steam billowed up through a hole in the floor near the front door, apparently from a boiler in the basement. The steam condensed on the concrete ceiling over the entranceway, then dripped back to the floor, creating small domes of ice that were guaranteed to break someone's leg. The only sure footing was provided by a carpet of cigarette butts.

The third-floor corridor was lit by one bulb. Our chilly room had three beds with extra blankets. Though the bathroom door down the hall was labeled with an M for "Moosh-SKOY" ("Men"), I discovered during my first visit that women also used these facilities. Perhaps the Ladies' Room was not functioning.

The lodge was equipped with a kitchen on the second floor which everyone was welcome to use. It had cold water and an electric stove that worked at two settings: OFF and HIGH. All its knobs were missing, so the intermediate settings were not available. We either plugged in the stove, or pulled out the plug.

Two homeless dogs, generally friendly, lived in the building. On Sunday morning, we found that the kitchen garbage from Saturday evening was strewn around the floor, nice to step over while preparing that first cup of instant coffee.

The meals, served in a large chilly dining hall overlooking the vast white expanse of the frozen Gulf, were prepared with professional care, though they were small. Our waitress did bring me a second bowl of porridge for breakfast, pleased that an American would like her "kasha". Two other tables were used by groups of skiers; most of the dining hall, which could easily seat two hundred people, was, like the lodge, virtually empty.

But it was our skis that told the story of Russia in 1996.

The ski shop was on the first floor of the lodge. The first-floor corridor had no light bulb at all, and was like a long black tunnel. We were able to locate the shop by the glow of light from beneath the door to one of the rooms. Opening the door, we discovered a room filled with racks of skis. We were greeted by a cheerful fellow named Nicholas, who was working with a screwdriver on a binding.

I knew my ski length in centimeters, for I had been skiing through the Norwegian mountains for the previous nine winters. Nicholas handed me two yellow skis of the right length. But when I inspected their bindings, I saw that both were labeled RIGHT, rather than RIGHT and LEFT. However, both ski tips were painted with number 98, so the skis were clearly intended to be a pair.

I waited for Nicholas to finish fitting Tanja with skis. She stepped into the bindings of one red ski, one blue ski. Looking more closely at the pairs of skis on the racks, I discovered that many pairs were made from skis of different colors: one usable ski had been combined with another usable ski. The shop was doing the best it could with the leftovers of better times.

When I pointed out to Nicholas that he had given me two right skis, he simply took them back and handed me another pair, both red, LEFT and RIGHT. I inspected their bottoms: bare chipped wood. The pine tar had been completely worn off, probably after the shop had run out of pine tar. I thanked Nicholas, (he smiled with pleasure at my Russian, and wished us a good trip,) then I took my skis outside, uncapped a stick of my green Norwegian wax and rubbed the bottoms of my antiques from end to end.

Nicholas waxed Tania's skis, and then Pavel's skis, with a stick of green which a skier last weekend had given him. It was the only wax he had in the shop. He was proud of his one stick because it was from Sweden.

As Tanja and I glided through a rolling forest of giant pines along the shore of the Gulf of Finland, where a scene from "Doctor Zhivago" could have been filmed, I noticed that the words printed in Cyrillic letters on the ends of her skis were not complete. Looking more closely, I saw that the ends of her skis had been cut off! No wonder they seemed so short. Their bindings had not been shifted: the front ends were of normal length, but the back ends were about a foot short.

I soon learned why her skis had been cut. One of my own skis began to drag. Its glide became increasingly rough. Finally I took it off to inspect its bottom, and discovered to my amazement that the ski was splitting from the rear end. The wood was so dry, the glue so old, that the ski was splitting into three separate layers as I used it.

The lodge was falling apart as we used it. The cold dirty bus we had ridden on was falling apart as we used it. So were most of the buses and trolley cars in St. Petersburg. So was the University where I taught, or now did not teach, for the building had been closed during the past two weeks because the heating system still had not been repaired. So many students and teachers had become sick from sitting day after day in rooms of 46°, that finally the dean had shut down the school.

I managed to glide and scrape, glide and scrape back to the ski shop. Nicholas shrugged, then gave me another pair, (my third,) both blue, LEFT and RIGHT, with bottoms of bare wood. Again I waxed from end to end. I am glad to report that I skied on that blue pair through Saturday afternoon and all day Sunday without any further problems. Nicholas skied with us on Sunday; a former coach, he skied on his Austrian fiberglass skis with the grace of a professional, and took us on a long, magnificent run through the hilly forest which we never would have found without him.

What was the cost of lodge, meals and ski rentals for one weekend? For two adults and a child, I paid 165,000 roubles, or $35. Roughly $12 per person. A bargain, certainly, were we at Stowe, Vermont. But we are in Russia, where the monthly salary of a university professor is about 200,000 roubles, or $42 per month, if the salaries are paid, which often they are not. So I had spent eighty-two percent of my monthly salary, not counting the cost of the Metro, the train and the bus, for our winter weekend.

Clearly, the lodge and dining hall were virtually empty because few people in St. Petersburg could afford such an extravagance.

EYES THAT ASK US THEIR QUESTION

I visited the many parks of St. Petersburg in every season, so I could watch the kids play in the bright leaves of autumn, and sled down the hills in winter, and chase each other in the warm sunshine of spring.

Likewise, I wanted to visit the war cemetery in all its moods. As a person may be drawn again and again to a certain Beethoven symphony, so I felt compelled to return again and again to St. Petersburg's symphony of silence.

On previous trips, I had ridden the Metro to Ploshchad Muzhestva, then bus 123 to the cemetery gate. But on this trip, two Metro stops before my stop, I heard an announcement which I did not understand, then I watched as everyone stood up and got out of the car. I recalled that part of the Metro line had recently flooded; some stations were closed. I walked out of the empty car, found a Metro attendant and asked her how I could get to Piskaryovskoye Memorial Cemetery. She told me to go up to the street and take bus 91. I thanked her and rode the escalator up to the street, but I found neither bus 91 nor anyone who had any idea where I might find that or any other bus to the cemetery. So I opened my map, falling apart at the seams, figured out a potential route, and began to walk along a snowy sidewalk.

However, the street names on my map were from the Soviet period and thus did not always correspond with the names posted (occasionally) on the streets themselves. When Leningrad changed its name back to St. Petersburg in 1991, many of the streets changed back to their pre-Revolutionary names as well. My Soviet map, which I had bought during my first trip in 1991, was hopelessly outdated.

Worse, the point where I now stood was the intersection of two folds on my map, so that most of the neighborhood was tattered and illegible. Glimpsing the Neva between two buildings, I turned my back to the river and so faced north, then I began to walk in a northerly direction along angling, curving, dead-ending streets, until I was, without benefit of the sun in the cloud-covered sky, completely lost.

I finally found a trolley stop, and there asked a woman bundled in a coat and scarf how to get to Piskaryovskoye Memorial Cemetery. My experience had often been that whenever I asked directions in my halting, stumblebum Russian, most citizens of St. Petersburg launched into a long and detailed answer, as if they not only wanted to tell me how to get there, but wished to provide me with the groundwork of a philosophical question which I might ponder along the way. This woman, however, must have met a lost American at least once before, because she held up her hand with five fingers, and then with one finger. Pointing up at a blue sign over the road that listed the numbers of the trolley cars which stopped here, she said 'fifty-one' in Russian while I spotted 51 in clear white numbers. I thanked her, and thanked her again as she climbed onto trolley 64. Before its door shut, she again held up five fingers, then one.

Trolley 51 came rattling along about twenty minutes later. Like most trolleys in St. Petersburg, it was not heated; the temperature inside was the same 5°F as the January day outside. The seats were filled, so I stood, gripping the overhead bar. Then I asked the woman standing beside me whether this trolley went to the gate of the cemetery. She was not sure. But other passengers had heard my question, and a discussion began among the people standing and seated around us. A man in a black overcoat touched my shoulder and indicated that he would tell me where to get off the trolley. I thanked him. Then I hunched down and peered through a small patch of clear glass in the frosted window which someone had scraped clean. We rattled northwards out of the old St. Petersburg and into a residential area with endless drab concrete apartment buildings. Had I tried to walk the entire distance, I would have spent hours trying to find my way through the snowy monolithic maze.

During the war, thousands of people had walked these kilometers northward, but they did not carry a trim backpack containing extra warm clothing and camera gear. They had pulled a body on a sled.

The man in a black overcoat showed me where to get off the trolley. When the door banged open, he stepped out onto the sidewalk with me and pointed down a broad boulevard that disappeared between gray buildings under a gray sky. "Five hundred meters," he told me, "on the right." Then he stepped back onto the trolley just before its door banged shut. Faces peered out from the frosted windows at me.

The Metro may lack the funds to repair a flooded station, but there certainly was no lack of kindness among the people of St. Petersburg.

One of Leningrad's poets, Sergei Davydov, wrote of Piskaryovskoye Cemetery, "Here lies half the city." No one knows how many people are buried in the mass graves, for the graves were simply giant trenches made by dynamiting the frozen ground; then frozen corpses in winter, and decomposing corpses in summer, were tumbled in. Estimates vary from eight hundred thousand to well over a million. Some of them were brought here by family members whose last effort was to trudge to this cemetery, and who then collapsed beside a father, a mother, a child. The next person to come along found the two frozen bodies at the edge of a pit.

Today, in January of 1996, the long mounds lay beneath a foot of snow, so that as I walked along the path toward the distant, snow-misted statue of the Motherland, I looked left and right at the ripples of two enormous white washboards. The stones at the ends of the mounds had been recently brushed by the gloves of previous visitors, though the dates, 1942, 1942, 1943, were veiled with a dusting of fresh white powder. The flowers which people had placed atop the stones were blanketed with snow; I could see the faint color of pink carnations, and of frozen red roses.

While I walked the long unshoveled path, following the footsteps of those who had been here before me today, I wondered how many composers lay silent beneath the snow, their scores forever unwritten because they had been children on the day a Nazi bomb crashed through the roof of their apartment buildings. How many future engineers lay here, five years old when their starved hearts stopped beating, who might have known how to repair a flooded Metro line? How many economists, how many ecologists, were buried in this sacred repository of wasted talent?

A month ago, just before Christmas, I went with a group of friends to hear a superb performance of Handel's "Messiah" in Smolny Cathedral. Both the choir and the orchestra were excellent. I especially enjoyed the moment after each movement when the musicians were silent, but the echo of their strings and voices came down from the cathedral's enormous dome, like an angelic echo from a distant heaven.

While I listened to Handel's anguished and contemplative and joyous music, I began to imagine that all of the violinists and the cellists and the trumpeters and the drummers who lay in the Piskaryovskoye earth were enabled tonight, in honor of the spirit of Christmas, to take their seats in the string section, and among the brass and woodwinds and percussion. They would bring with them not only their musical skills, but a heightened spiritual understanding, a deepened appreciation, which would result from their having missed over fifty Christmases. I wished that the adequate but less-than-exultant choir might be afforded the voices of another five hundred members: the bass voices of men who had stood their ground in the bloody trenches that had guarded the gates of Leningrad; the tenor voices of men who had driven trucks laden with flour and medicine across the ice of Lake Ladoga on the Road of Life, while Nazi planes swooped down and strafed them; the alto voices of women who had continued to teach in the schools, although their pupils disappeared one by one; and the soprano voices of women who had worked in dark hospitals without heat, then went home to dark apartments without heat to see if their own mothers and children were still alive.

Yes, I wished to augment those voices ranged in a horseshoe behind the orchestra in Smolny Cathedral that night. I wanted to add the high, bright, silvery voices of a children's choir, so that Handel's jubilant music might be imbued with their boundless hope and unfettered exultation, with their immediate and untutored belief in the Christmas spirit, with their innocent joy.

I would have liked, during the moment of silence after each musical movement, to have heard those extra celestial voices ringing down from the great dome above us.

In Piskaryovskoye Cemetery on that cold gray January day, I came to the end of the path and looked up at the tall dark statue of the Motherland, wearing on her shoulders and outstretched arms a mantle of white.

I wished that she might step down from her pedestal, and walk with firm strides across the flat expanse of northern Russia from St. Petersburg to Moscow, where she would enter the Parliament in which the old men squabbled. Speaking for her people who could no longer speak, she would ask the politicians, "In whose interest are you bickering today? In whose interest are you scheming and intriguing? In whose interest are you fighting your war in Chechnya? To what purpose are the young men coming home dead today in the back of Russian trucks?"

"What," she would ask, "have you old men ever learned about war, about peace?"

I walked through a section of the cemetery where, beneath tall white birch trees, their branches black against the low gray sky, people had been buried in individual graves during the war. I knelt and brushed the snow from one of the stones that lay flat, and found a black-and-white photograph of a face, printed on an oval of white porcelain. This is a tradition in Russia: on the cross or monument, there may be a picture of the person who is buried here. I looked at the face of a man named Sakarov, who wore an old-fashioned flat cap. He had died at the age of twenty-two in 1941, when most American men had not yet heard of a Navy base named Pearl Harbor.

I walked a short distance along a path, then knelt again and brushed the snow from the somber face of a man who died in 1942, when he was thirty-three years old. His name was on the stone, but not the cause of his death. He might have been a soldier in the front-line trenches ringing the city; he might have been a passenger on a trolley car rattling along Nevsky Prospect when an artillery shell hit; he might have been a skeletal victim of starvation who froze to death in bed with an uncle, a brother, a son whom he was trying to keep warm.

Some of the sepia-toned photographs were affixed to upright stones, so that the eyes of the dead peered at the world from just above the layer of snow. The nose and cheeks were buried by white powder, but the eyes could stare into the land of the living and ask their questions. The names were hidden beneath the snow, the dates were hidden, but the eyes of painters and poets, of professors and pediatricians, looked at me and asked, "How fare the people to whom we hoped to give a new and better world?"

Chapter Eight

SNAPSHOTS AND VIGNETTES

On a clear winter's night, Orion peered down into the courtyard outside my window. He was striding with his usual vigor in pursuit of some celestial prey, and his bright-eyed hound was bounding close behind him. They paused for a moment, a long moment, for there was much to see in a boxed-in courtyard in St. Petersburg.

Peeking over the rooftops, Orion watched an old woman as she tossed a broken crate onto a heap of burning trash. She went back to the garbage bin and pulled out anything that would burn: cardboard boxes, several milk cartons, an orange juice carton. Walking back and forth, she tossed them into the fire. The rumpled silver lining from the orange juice carton rose in the smoke, then drifted down and landed in the court where the boys played soccer: a bit more trash for them to ignore.

Orion was curious, as he looked down at this terrestrial world: Why was the old woman burning trash from a garbage bin at ten o'clock at night?

Because the city of St. Petersburg does not have the money to hire a truck to collect the garbage; and if she, a devoted Soviet worker who for fifty years has never shirked her duty to her country, does not try every night to burn at least a portion of the daily trash, then the bin will overflow and the children's football court will become a dump. The rats will greatly outnumber the cats. Wild dogs will come to forage, and to fight. Unpaid, unsupervised, unasked, she does her nightly job.

Orion's hound, its eye the brightest star in the southern sky, stared down at a cat sitting near the warm fire. She gnawed on chicken bones which the old woman had brought her. If any dogs came, the woman would chase them away with a stick.

Orion turned his attention to a man trying to start his car. The dry cranking of the starter motor alternated with the sudden roar of a badly tuned engine at full throttle; then the engine died. A pause followed, while the man got out of his car, leaned over the engine, (lit by a glow of light from the auto repair shop,) and tinkered with its innards. Now the man sat once more behind the wheel, and a small brief flame appeared as he lit a cigarette. Orion listened to the dry cranking, cranking, cranking of the starter motor, (the battery was weakening,) followed by the sudden rattling roar of the engine at the verge of exploding. But once again the engine abruptly stopped, filling the courtyard with a moment of lovely silence.

Until, as if nudged to life by the engine's rattle-bang-BOOM!, an alarm in a nearby car began to wail. Orion searched to see who was burgling the car. No one. As usual, no one. The man smoking his cigarette did not bother even to turn his head toward the repetitious electronic shrieking. It was one of several car alarms that would blast and scream and wail tonight at some random hour, for some unknown reason. If these alarms really signaled that someone was stealing a car, all the vehicles parked below would have been gone months ago.

Orion worries:

What about the nails in that burning crate, left in the ashes near the soccer court?

Will the woman manage to have chicken bones for the cat tomorrow night?

Couldn't a truck come at least *once* during the winter to pick up the garbage?

And why, WHY, *WHY*, Orion and I would like to know, do those car alarms send their frenzied cry up to a thousand apartment windows, and up to the heavens as well, a dozen times in the course of a night? If not alarms, are they anguished prayers of despair?

Along a blackened path through the snow walked a girl, carrying a satchel. At ten minutes after ten, she was perhaps returning from a friend's apartment, where they had worked on their mathematics together. The black path crossed through the glow of amber light from the auto repair shop, then wound past the battered fence of the soccer court, and continued close to the garbage bin, close to the fire.

From my sixth-floor window, I could see Orion watching the girl. But down in the courtyard, walled in by brick and concrete buildings, the girl could not see Orion and his handsome hound on their evening jaunt across the southern sky. She could see the blinking yellow parking lights of the car with the blaring alarm. She could see the man leaning over his engine. She could see the rubbish burning. She could see the cat licking its paw. And she could see a babushka poking a stick into the garbage bin.

Will her teacher give her an A tomorrow on her mathematics exercises?

Orion strode west toward the Gulf of Finland, toward the clean streets of Helsinki, toward the quiet courtyards of Stockholm. The Great Hound leapt eagerly westward toward the tall, silent, snow-covered mountains of Norway.

Though I had visited art museums and attended symphony concerts wherever in my peripatetic life I have lived, I discovered something new and wonderful in the ever surprising city of St. Petersburg. Never before had I been in the presence of so many children walking through the galleries, or sitting with their families in Symphony Hall. Russian apartments are small, courtyards are cluttered, and schools are modestly equipped; however, the children of St. Petersburg are encouraged by their teachers and parents to let their minds explore far beyond the limits of their dingy day-to-day surroundings. Nurtured by a world which even the Bolsheviks failed to destroy, giggling ten-year-olds and gangly teenagers return again and again to their favorite paintings in the Hermitage and the Russian Museum. With a sixteenth birthday coming, boys as well as girls truly do ask if Papa could buy tickets to a ballet in which Tchaikovsky's magical fairy tale makes perfect and beautiful sense.

The museums and concert halls are St. Petersburg's other schools. They impart a rich and fascinating education which nourishes that fabled Russian soul. In my own classroom, if I referred during a discussion in English to a certain sculpture or painting in a museum, virtually every student was familiar with it. If I referred to some aspect of Russian history, as portrayed by Pushkin or set to music by Tchaikovsky, my seventeen-year-olds (with bluejeans and adolescent skin,) knew the story so well that they would fill in the details for the teacher. What a profound pleasure, for a burnt-out professor who had spent too many years trying to awaken young American minds that thrived on basketball personalities, computer games, TV sitcoms, and videos of Rauncho III, to spend an hour in class with kids who not only knew their history and culture, but were deeply proud of both.

Ekaterina, my colleague at the University, loved to take me through the Hermitage, where she could show me the paintings she had especially liked as a child. A Dutch still life of a butchered beef carcass had caught her fancy. She stared with perhaps a bit of lingering envy at portraits of the aristocracy in their military uniforms and elegant gowns. Her favorite painting had been the huge, apocalyptic picture of "The Last Day of Pompei", by the Russian artist Karl Bryullov. I thus walked through the galleries of the Hermitage with both a gifted linguist and a wonder-struck child.

And then, while we gazed up at a painting in one of the sumptuously gilded rooms, I would turn with a smile toward the door, for I could hear the chatter and shuffle of an approaching group of school children, led by a museum guide and followed by one or two teachers. The guide was brimming with enthusiasm as she assembled her flock in front of Rembrandt's "The Prodigal Son". The kids were attentive— yes, truly attentive—as she pointed out the expression of forgiveness on the old man's face, then pointed at the son's torn clothing and bare foot. The teachers were gratefully silent as they rested their eyes on Rembrandt's deep and peaceful browns.

Katya's favorite sculpture was in a long gallery of figures. As a girl, she had admired the white marble body of Able as he lay on his back, lifeless, slain a moment ago by his brother Cain.

The sculpture gallery was filled with perfect bodies, male and female, adorned, if at all, with a bit of drapery or a fig leaf. Perhaps the teenagers who moved slowly from figure to figure paid less attention to the guide's lecture on the myth of Cupid and Psyche, than they did to the fact that he's grabbing her breast.

Katya's favorite room in the Hermitage, the Peacock Clock Room, was so ornate that to enter it was like walking into a jewel box. Its white walls ornamented with gold, its windows looking out on the Neva River, here was surely where Cinderella had danced with her Prince.

One of the most popular rooms in the Hermitage was the armor exhibit, where knights fully equipped with swords and lances sat upon stuffed horses. Ranks of old firearms, pikes and scimitars filled the window displays. Even the most dull-eyed schoolboy, dragged by his teacher from room to room to look at all this "old stuff", perked up as he examined a pair of dueling pistols. The next time he reads about Pushkin's death, he'll remember those big-barrelled weapons.

St. Petersburg is the city that sent Tchaikovsky to New York in 1891 for the opening of Carnegie Hall; the great composer conducted his own works, then took the train to visit Niagara Falls. And St. Petersburg is the city that now produces Leonard Bernstein's "West Side Story", with Tony and Maria singing in Russian.

This is a generous, wise and compassionate city, where music lovers can enter the elegant theater in one of the old aristocratic palaces, then listen to a concert performed by ten- and twelve-year-old students. I heard an extraordinary violin solo, played by a boy about four feet tall, with a round, Mongolian face; the music he performed was both complex and vibrant. I listened to a young girl with blond curls, who sat on a cushion on the piano bench so she could reach the keys; her cadenzas were powerful and professional. And I listened to a duet, brother on the piano and sister on the cello; they passed a melodic phrase back and forth, each time developing it further, as if they played an intricate and challenging game of catch.

What was most stunning about this children's concert was the fact that the music they were pouring out was not written by Tchaikovsky or Mussorgsky or Chopin, but by these kids themselves.

At the end of each performance, a dozen beaming admirers walked down the aisle to the stage with bouquets of flowers for the shy, elated youngster who tonight was a star.

This is a city with a congenial circus. After each act, children walked boldly down the steep steps and right into the ring, where they handed their flowers to the acrobats and clowns. One little girl will forever remember the night she offered her handful of pink carnations to the curling trunk of a huge gray elephant.

And this is a city where a lovelorn woman can go home from a concert happy. A young man with flowing dark hair and kind eyes played his guitar at the edge of the stage. After he was finished singing her favorite Russian ballad, she could walk up to the stage and hand him a bouquet of red roses with her secret message rolled up tightly and hidden among the stems. That message will forever gladden her heart, for she would know that after the concert, he held the sheet of paper in his exquisite hands and read her shy, honest, passionate words.

On the other hand:

On an early visit to St. Petersburg, I did a dumb thing which I haven't done since. Walking late at night from the Metro to my hotel, I decided that rather than follow a route of nondescript streets, I would walk along the Neva's embankment, where I would have a splendid view of the city lights reflected on the glossy black river. I was amply rewarded: the blue-white sparks in the wires above a trolley car crossing a bridge reflected like twin flashes of fireworks. I could hear the waves washing along the embankment wall, and the occasional bump and crunch of chunks of ice. The wintry air was clean and cold, blowing over the city from the Gulf, a wonderful relief after the warm stuffy air of the Metro.

I heard rapid footsteps behind me, following. Glancing over my shoulder, I saw a man about fifty feet behind me, walking fast. I walked more quickly, but heard that he was catching up. Peering over the wall at jagged gray sheets of ice in the black water, I realized what a fool I was to be walking here. Should he manage to stick a knife into me, grab my wallet and toss me over the wall, I wouldn't last half a minute in that frigid water. How many other such fools now rolled their bones along the bottom?

Now I saw a car coming in the opposite direction, moving very slowly, with several people in it.

Otherwise, the street in both directions was deserted.

"Pardon, pardon," said the man just behind me. I turned to face him. With a cigarette in his mouth, he gestured to ask if I had a match.

"Nyet," I said curtly, backing away. The car stopped ten feet from us, doors swung open and three men jumped out. The guy with the cigarette grabbed my arm. Spinning, I yanked my arm free, then dashed across the empty street, getting at least away from the river. Footsteps chased after me, but few Russians are joggers, and few joggers were fueled by the fear that drove my feet at full sprint, even in snow boots. Gripping the straps of my backpack while I raced along an icy sidewalk, I glanced back and saw four men returning to their car. Would they make a U-turn and follow? "Get the hell oughta here!" I roared at them in English.

Running the length of a deserted city block, I searched for anyone else out in the street, looked for even a truck or a bus. No one. Glancing back, I saw with enormous relief that the car had vanished. Slowing my pace slightly, I ran until I reached the hotel's front door.

The doorman, recognizing me, unlocked the heavy glass door and let me in. He stared at me as I stood panting in the lobby. Well-protected against the January cold in my red L.L. Bean down jacket, I was soaked with sweat.

From the window of my hotel room, I stared down at the silent black river. I knew in my still-thumping heart that by day this was a city of hunger, by night a city of fear.

During the winter of 1995/96, the banks were operating in a fairly reliable manner, but no one was taking any chances. Every time I went to the neighborhood bank to exchange dollars (in traveler's checks) into roubles, I had to wait in a small guarded room just inside the front door, because customers were allowed into the bank lobby only one at a time. While I waited, (and read a copy of Leon Trotsky's "The Russian Revolution",) I was watched by several guards who wore bullet-proof vests and carried short automatic rifles.

Once, when I sat down in a vacant chair, a guard sat down beside me and laid his rifle across his lap, its barrel pointed carelessly at my stomach. The little round bore was inches from my red jacket. What if I had gestured with my thumb toward his rifle and asked, 'Say, would you mind pointing that thing toward the ceiling?' Would he have pumped a couple of slugs into me, just to be on the safe side?

Fortunately another guard soon waved to me from the door to the lobby. Before I moved, I called a loud and clear 'Thank you' to him in Russian, ("Spah-SEE-bah",) then I nodded to the guard seated beside me, who nodded back with equal courtesy. I stood up from my chair and walked through the door into the large marble lobby, vacant except for the armed guards who kept their eye on me. The mirrors evenly spaced around the walls of the lobby were not for combing one's hair; they were one-way windows, and should the hired boys fail to stop any mischief, no doubt the heavies were ready and waiting to spring into action.

I approached the exchange window, a mouse hole ten inches long and four inches high, so low and small that I could not see the face of the woman who would change my money. I saw her hand as she took my traveler's check and blue American passport. Five minutes later, I saw her hand again as she passed through the rectangular hole a receipt, my passport, and a thick bundle of Russian bills.

"Thank you," I said in Russian toward the mouse hole.

I heard her reply in Russian, "You are welcome."

On a Sunday morning, Ekaterina and I took the train south to the nearby town of Pushkin, where we planned to spend the afternoon visiting the Catherine Palace, the summer home of Catherine the Great, and one of the largest palaces in the world. The long, three-story, sumptuously ornate building, blue with white trim, stands in a large wooded park. The five golden onion domes which cap the palace's built-in church rise above the crowns of oak and spires of spruce.

Katya and I decided, before we entered the palace, to walk through the fresh snow in the park. The white birches were bare of leaves, the brown tamaracks had lost their needles, and the huge black oaks reached their limbs, on which clung a few rustling brown leaves, into a brooding wintry sky.

Here in this park, while Washington was commanding his bedraggled army against the British redcoats, Catherine the Great had strolled with her aristocratic courtiers.

We met a man who was not strolling, but making his way slowly with a cane, its tip leaving evenly-spaced holes in the snow. Bundled in an old overcoat, his weathered face capped by a fur hat, he was glad to talk with us. He taught me the names of the trees in Russian, and I learned that tamaracks, also known as larches in English, have two names in Russian too.

After a pause, the three of us standing quietly in the lightly falling snow, he told us that he was alone. He had lost his wife three years ago. They had lost their only child, a son of twenty-eight, ten years ago: he was killed in Afghanistan.

One of my best friends in high school, the captain of our swimming team, had come home from Vietnam in a body bag. In my heart, how close I was to this Russian man; yet in our lives, how distant.

The old gentleman asked in Russian, "And for what?"

Let Brezhnev answer. Let McNamara answer.

And for what?

As I walked home one afternoon through a neighborhood park, I noticed a black-and-white cat sleeping on a manhole cover. The cat's fur was damp, for steam seeped from around the edge of the warm cover. The cat seemed to float on a brown raft in a sea of snow. Someone had placed bits of food on the manhole cover: chunks of bread, pieces of what appeared to be some sort of meat, and a small heap of spaghetti noodles.

I had never noticed this manhole cover before, though I had walked through the park almost every day. Perhaps the flow of hot water in the sewer below was only temporary. When the water stopped flowing, and the steam stopped heating the cover, would the damp cat freeze to the disk of cold steel in her sleep?

I was riding up a long steep Metro escalator, breathing warm stale air, my eyes closed with exhaustion. I had spent the entire afternoon trying to cash a traveler's check in one, two, three different Russian banks, and then at two hotels. I had failed everywhere because I did not have (as required by a new law) my receipt from the bank in Boonville, New York, where I had purchased the checks two years ago.

My foot on the sinking step ahead of me told me that I was approaching the top of the escalator. I opened my weary eyes, stepped off the moving belt and noticed a filthy dog with matted brown fur standing just to one side of the flow of people. It stood unsteadily, with dull eyes. From its mouth jutted a yellow chicken's foot.

After the collapse of the Soviet Union in 1991, many people were forced by their desperate situation to put their dogs and cats out in the street, for they could not afford to feed them. Family pets wandered lost in city traffic. Dogs gathered in packs that lived in wooded parks, and foraged in courtyard dumps for food. The melting snow in the spring revealed dead cats in the bushes, dead dogs along the curb.

One winter evening, after visiting friends in their apartment, I took the elevator down to the lobby. As I stepped out of the elevator into an entryway lit by one bulb, a woman in a snowy overcoat and scarf stepped in through the front door. Over her arm was draped what looked to be a dead cat. But the cat was not quite dead, she explained, showing me that its eyes were still partly open. If she warmed it, and fed it, and gave it a bath, it might survive. She already had three cats and two dogs up in her apartment, all of which she had found half-frozen outside. She collected chicken bones from her neighbors. It was the best she could do.

―――――――――

Jogging along the Fontanka River one evening, (when the traffic was light and the air was a bit cleaner,) I saw a man pushing another man along the street in a wheelchair. The chrome rim of the right wheel rippled back and forth as the chair rolled along: the wheel was badly bent, as if the chair had been hit by a car.

The sidewalk was uneven, occasionally broken, often caked with ice. The snow and ice on the street, however, had been worn away by the day's traffic. So the man in the wheelchair rolled along in the street.

Two weeks later, again in the evening, though on the other side of the river, that same wheel caught my eye. In the glow of a streetlamp, it was undulating like a silver jellyfish.

―――――――――

Once in St. Petersburg, I became as angry as I have ever been in my life.

I was on a two-week visit from Norway in 1994, and I had brought twelve boxes of books, to be distributed at both the University and at School #11. Since the beginning of our program in 1991, the Graduate School of Business in Bodø had provided over $10,000 worth of funding for books in the fields of business and economics. Some were American textbooks, others were British Broadcasting Company books from London, especially designed for foreigners learning Business English. In addition, a Norwegian friend of mine living in Bergen often contributed a box of books, such as dictionaries for the classrooms. Further, my parents annually sent several boxes of children's books to me in Norway, and then I would take them on to St. Petersburg. Scandinavian Airlines helped enormously by charging their lowest fee possible for air freight, when the heavy boxes of books accompanied me on the plane from Bodø to Oslo, and then from Oslo to St. Petersburg. Thus we had an excellent system: Norwegian and American generosity enabled a steady stream of books to enter the classrooms of two schools in Russia, where several hundred students could read them.

The problem was at the airport in St. Petersburg, where I had to take the books through customs. Though these were "school books for the children of Russia," the customs officials demanded a fee equal to half of the value of the books, to be paid with American dollars. I was astonished. On previous trips I had experienced only minimal difficulties in bringing books through customs, but now the bandits wanted over a thousand dollars in American cash. Though I argued vehemently with several officials, (while the head of the foreign language department at the University waited for me in the lobby, watching the altercation through a glass wall,) I was allowed to take only my two suitcases, but no boxes of books.

During the following week, the dean of the University phoned the customs office; but the books would not be released until payment of the appropriate fee. At my urgent request, the American Consulate phoned the customs office, explaining that the books were "humanitarian aid"; but the books would not be released until payment of the appropriate fee. I needed these books for my two weeks of teaching, and already we had lost a full week. Further, I knew that if I returned to Norway before I managed to get the books to the University and School #11, neither school would ever see them, and all the future courses I had planned would collapse. The boys at customs would simply channel the books into the black market: textbooks and children's books and dictionaries would all appear for sale on the street.

So Alexandra, the head of the foreign language department, a determined Russian who had dealt with crisis after crisis at her virtually bankrupt University, borrowed a large cargo truck, battered and blue, with a driver who drove it as if he were battalion commander of a legion of armored tanks. Alexandra, Yuri and I, seated together in the cab as an indomitable troika, headed for the airport.

Alexandra and I entered the customs office, while Yuri waited in the truck at the gate to the pick-up yard. The staff in the front office, at two in the afternoon, had closed the window for their half-hour tea break. At least twenty Russians were waiting in the lobby for the window to re-open. We waited.

When the window finally slid open, six minutes after the end of the half-hour tea break, a blank face stared out. The throng crowded forward. I could see that we would stand at the outer periphery for at least an hour before we managed to push our way to that window. So I found a door and pounded on it.

When an infuriated official opened it, I insisted in English that I speak at once with the Director of Customs. When he snapped back in Russian and began to close the door, I slammed my fist against the door frame and thundered at him that he would have the American ambassador in his office within one hour, with an American police escort, if I did not speak immediately with the Director. I doubt he followed much of what I said, but he clearly did understand that he had one of those berserk American Rambo crazies on his hands, who might well be back in half an hour with a Star Wars cannon. Rather than confront me any further, better to pass me on to the Director.

"Syih-CHAHS," he said, 'Wait a moment,' then he tried to close the door. I held it open with my shoulder and my boot. He made a phone call, then he silently escorted Alexandra and I down a dusty cluttered hallway to the Director's office, a dusty, cluttered, windowless, smoke-filled room where The Heavy sat behind his desk heaped with papers which had probably been moldering there since his great-grandfather first held the Directorship in 1918. I shook hands, then sat in a chair and stared him square in the eye while Alexandra explained that the books were not for sale, but for our students at the University.

After ten minutes, it was clear that, despite Alexandra's commendable combination of restraint and firmness, we had not budged the Bulky Bureaucrat even a quarter of an inch. He was explaining that even humanitarian aid was subject to the fee structure at the custom's office. That was the law. He shrugged. That was the law.

I was shaking with rage. I had read in novels about people shaking with rage, and now I was doing it. Not just my hands; my whole body.

With a teacher's stentorian voice, able to reach to the last row of a large university auditorium with a boom that silenced the chatterers and awoke the dead, I pointed a pistol-barrel finger at him and shouted, "Now you listen to me."

I doubt he knew more than two words of English, but as I poured out my fury at the slimy bunch of corrupt bastards who were keeping the good, honest, hard-working students and teachers of Russia from getting on with the job of building a *real* country, rather than this shameful hog sty where he was wallowing up to his filthy ears, El Supremo began to realize that today he was going to earn his pay, rather than steal it. When he tried to speak, I slammed my fist on his desk, then roared that when he and his ilk were finally put where they belonged, he would have all the books he wanted in the prison library.

When Big Turd raised his voice, I was on my feet. Setting two fists on his desk, I leaned forward until my face was glaring down at his, and told him that I wanted full payment for a week's wasted time at the professorial wage of fifty dollars an hour, plus payment for the time I was wasting on this Monday afternoon, and that I wanted that payment in one-hundred dollar bills in American cash, and that I wanted it NOW.

The next step was obvious: I was going to pick up his desk, lift it over my head, then bring it crashing down on top of him.

He picked up one of his three phones, said a few words, set the phone down and told Alexandra that we could pick up our books at Building Number Five.

"Thank you," she said.

I said, "I will inspect every box. If so much as a coloring book is missing, *you* will pay."

He gestured toward the door: we were welcome to leave now.

Alexandra picked up a written pass at the front office, then took it out to Yuri, so he could bring his truck into the yard. I stayed *inside* the building, and insisted that I be escorted directly to Building Number Five. They were not going to get rid of me until I drove away with those books.

After a bit of searching in a warehouse heaped to the ceiling with what were essentially stolen goods, I located the dozen boxes with my handwriting on them, stating BOOKS in Russian, Norwegian and English. While I watched, an official opened two of the boxes to ascertain that the contents really were books. Then I opened the other ten boxes, to ascertain that the bastards hadn't stolen anything.

Everything was in order: the entire inventory as I had carefully packed it, including twenty copies of *The Pokey Little Puppy*, and multiple copies of articles from *The Economist* which I had Xeroxed in Norway. We would now have a very busy second week, but at least we had the books.

While Alexandra signed papers, Yuri and I loaded the dozen boxes into the truck. The big, blue, battered, rumbling monster could have held a hundred boxes, maybe two hundred boxes. Next time. Perhaps I would even make a personal phone call to the Director, letting him know that my shipment was on its way.

The troika climbed up into the cab, then we rumbled out of the courtyard and through the gate, onto the potholed highway toward the city, with our load of gold bullion in the back.

Let us turn now to the true heroes of Russia today, her teachers.

I heard many times from many different people during my visits to Russia, that the Soviet system had destroyed everything but the schools. "Why," I asked, "did the schools manage to survive so well?"

"Because of the teachers. Because of the school directors."

Most of whom, at the grade school and high school level, were women. Who focused on the needs of the children.

If America truly wanted to build a solid peace with our Cold War enemy, then our high schools from Maine to California should each invite a Russian teacher of English to visit them for at least one full semester, better the entire year. Our guest could teach Russian, of course, and she could contribute to history and social studies classes, but her real job would be fourfold:

1. to improve her English with the help of American teachers of English;

2. to learn about teaching methods in the American classroom;

3. to select books in English for her classrooms and library in Russia;

4. to become trained in the basics of e-mail, so that when she returns home, she will be able to provide a link of direct communication between Russian students and American students. Then, for the first time in the history of our two nations, our young people can learn from each other, and can build a network of friendship, an ever-growing mutual understanding, and thus a true foundation for peace.

What, budgets are tight? We're all too busy, too overworked already? Let the diplomats and the politicians build the peace?

When the Founding Fathers wrote, "We the People," they meant it.

Chapter Nine

THE 50TH ANNIVERSARY OF VICTORY DAY

On May 9, 1995, the people of Russia celebrated the 50th anniversary of their victory over Nazi Germany. The citizens of St. Petersburg looked back half a century to their most savage ordeal, the 900-day siege; and at the same time, they looked forward to the long-awaited day when their children and grandchildren might finally enjoy the full blessings of peace and prosperity.

Following World War II, Japan and much of Germany became open to Americans. We could travel in both countries, we could communicate with our former enemies, and thus we could try to understand their viewpoints and their cultures.

However, our most powerful wartime ally, the Soviet Union, the other half of the vise that ultimately crushed Berlin, became closed to Americans after 1945. We could not travel to Leningrad to talk with the survivors about their ordeal, nor could we help them to rebuild their city. We could not visit classrooms to learn the lessons of history as Russian children learned them. We could not meet again and share a congenial beer with the Soviet soldiers who had closed ranks with American troops on the banks of the Elbe River. We could not lend a helping hand, nor offer an understanding ear. All further communication was prohibited, because the Soviet people, who lost more men, women and children to the ravages of war than any other nation, were locked inside Stalin's impenetrable prison.

After nearly half a century of mutual threats and mutual ignorance, Mikhail Gorbachev opened the prison doors. In 1991, the Russians were at last able to peer out at the world, and teachers like myself were welcomed into their classrooms. The two blindfolded antagonists with nuclear knives at each other's throats, finally laid their knives on the table and took off their blindfolds.

I was determined to be in St. Petersburg during the week leading up to Victory Day, 1995, and on that extraordinary day itself. I was curious: How would the Russians feel on the 50th anniversary of their military triumph? Would they strut with rifles and flags, and parade their artillery and rocket launchers, in an effort to revive their glory days as a superpower? Would they shake their fist at the memory of Nazi Germany? Would they acknowledge, or would they ignore, their Western allies?

Fifty years ago, the citizens of Leningrad struggled to rebuild their demolished city. Today, the citizens of St. Petersburg struggled to rebuild their demolished economy. What sort of victory could people living under today's grim conditions be able to celebrate?

During the week leading up to the 9th of May, Russian battleships rode at anchor on the Neva in the heart of the city. Trimmed with bright flags, the giant gray ships enabled veterans to remember the pride they once felt in their nation's military strength. During recent months, the Russian army had shown the world an appalling lack of professionalism as it bombed the capital of Chechnya into rubble, and sent thousands of poorly trained young soldiers to their deaths. Few Russians were proud of what their misguided government was doing in that pointless war. However, the veterans of Leningrad were deeply proud of what they themselves had done when they kept the fascists from entering the gates of their city. Through three northern winters, they did not give up. The fleet of battleships gathered this week on the Neva, the river that had carried away so many of their dead, reminded the old soldiers of the time when their courage and determination were unsurpassed in all the world.

A woman of seventy stood at the granite embankment wall with a bouquet of red carnations. She stared out at a warship. Had she lost her husband, her brother, her father to the flames of war? Quite possibly, she had lost all three. And now, fifty years after the Soviet Union's costly victory, how did she feel that the Soviet Union no longer existed?

A grandfather took a picture of his three grinning grandchildren on the sunny embankment; an angular ship with huge guns floated on the steel-blue river in the background. Proud of the ship, proud of his grandchildren, today he was a happy man. This picture he took: it was as much for the trio of well-dressed kids twenty years from now, as it was for him today.

On Nevsky Prospect, the city's main boulevard, a blue sign with white letters was still painted (and freshly repainted) on the facade of a building on the northern side of the street. First painted during the siege, it warned people, "During artillery shelling, this side is more dangerous." The opposite, southern side of the boulevard was protected by buildings from German artillery shells fired from the south; pedestrians should walk on that side, where, except at the cross streets, they would be safer.

During the week leading up to Victory Day, this blue sign, maintained as a memorial for fifty years, was almost obscured behind bouquets of fresh flowers.

All around the city, colorful banners draped across the streets and on lampposts commemorated the Victory. But while the Russians were celebrating, they were also enduring a deep and unrelenting grief.

During the week before the 9th of May, families visited Piskaryovskoye Memorial Cemetery in an endless stream to honor the dead. On the 8th of May, a drizzle fell from low clouds, muting the fresh spring-green of the grass. People carried umbrellas in one hand and flowers in the other as they entered the gate and stood reverently before the eternal flame.

In a steady procession of multi-colored umbrellas, families walked along the gravel path, past the long grass-covered mounds filled with people who had once walked the streets of Leningrad. Families paused, their umbrellas touching like a cluster of mushrooms, so that children could place a flower on the dated gray stones that said so little, that said so much.

At the end of the long path, families climbed the stone steps until they stood before the towering figure of the Motherland. Around her pedestal lay a dozen large flowered wreaths, the messages on their ribbons in Cyrillic. I noticed one ribbon with Latin letters, and discovered that the wreath had been placed here by people from Hamburg, Germany. I knew enough German to read, "Never again." People from Hamburg had come on a pilgrimage of repentance, and the citizens of St. Petersburg had allowed them to enter a shrine forever sacred.

I noticed an old woman who wore a long black coat and carried a pink umbrella. She had placed her flowers at the foot of the Motherland, and now she walked back along the path toward the spark of flickering orange flame. She paused at each stone, 1944, 1943, 1942, 1941; holding the pink umbrella with one hand, she placed her other hand flat upon every stone. Perhaps a sister was buried here somewhere, and to be sure that her sister felt her touch, the woman laid her hand on each stone.

Or perhaps the woman was touching all who slept here, the million souls for whom the last lullaby had been the blast of a bomb.

On Tuesday, the 9th of May, 1995, all of Russia celebrated Victory Day. On Tuesday, the 9th of May, 1995, all of Russia mourned Victory Day.

In a television documentary at ten a.m. on Tuesday morning, reporters interviewed a special group of veterans: men and women who had spent the past fifty years as invalids in military hospitals. These veterans now had the opportunity to reminisce, to philosophize, to complain, to blame: to state the truth as they saw it. Never before had I witnessed on television such a mix of brutal reality and stoic dignity.

At eleven a.m., the people of Leningrad/St. Petersburg watched their televisions as new wreaths were laid at the foot of the Motherland. The camera slowly scanned the long green mounds while somber music played in the background. I sat with a Russian family in their living room. Not since watching John Kennedy's funeral on television had I felt the profound grief of a nation in mourning.

During the afternoon, virtually every person in Russia visited a cemetery. In St. Petersburg, the birches were just putting out their glossy green leaves beneath a pale blue sky, as families gathered to clean a grave, to plant fresh flowers, and perhaps to eat a little bread and to toast with vodka in memory of the twenty-seven million Soviet victims of war.

A lone woman sat on a bench beside a grave and stared down at the earth, in prayer, in pain.

Another woman followed a Russian tradition: she spread bird seed on the headstone of her brother's grave. Perhaps, during his twenty-one years, he had enjoyed hearing the song of finches in the garden.

An old soldier with a row of medals on his jacket walked with a limp through a small neighborhood cemetery. He held the hand of a boy of five who walked with solemn dignity. Together, they placed flowers beside a memorial to a dozen children who, while they had been walking together home from school, were hit by an artillery shell.

Their names were inscribed on the memorial; the old soldier read each name to the boy.

I could not help thinking about our Veterans' Day in America, on November 11. The post offices and other government buildings were closed, but most stores were open for business as usual. Certainly, during the week leading up to Veterans' Day, no veterans were ever honored at my school.

Our Memorial Day at the end of May is often picnic day, the summer kick-off, the first three-day weekend after a long winter. Time to open the summer cottage, time to launch the boat. Our annual car race, the Indianapolis 500, would be unthinkable in Russia. TV coverage of changing tires during a pit stop in less than twenty seconds, the oily flames of a spectacular crash, the giant beer bash in the parking lot: to the Russians, such doings on a sacred day appear as barbaric.

In the afternoon on Victory Day, the veterans of the Great Patriotic War paraded along the boulevards of their cities and towns and villages throughout Russia.

There was no fist-shaking at Nazi Germany.

There was no waving of flags from America or England or France.

As I watched the parade in St. Petersburg, I saw no tanks, no artillery, no jets roaring overhead. I didn't see a single rifle. The parade moving slowly along Nevsky Prospect consisted of men and women in their sixties and seventies and some in their eighties. Many of them carried flowers; some walked with a cane. Some of the veterans wore a full uniform, while most wore their medals on a civilian jacket.

Fifty years ago in the Soviet armed forces, women had piloted fighter planes, women had manned anti-aircraft guns, women had fought from trench to trench all the way to Berlin. Today, a large portion of the soldiers walking along the boulevard between cheering crowds were proud, strong, gray-haired women, wearing brightly colored medals on a jacket over a dress.

One group in the parade, men and women in their fifties, carried a banner that proclaimed, CHILDREN OF THE BLOCKADE. Their childhood had been a time of bombs and starvation and family deaths, but they had survived. As they moved in a group up Nevsky, a loud, continuous cheer followed them.

Some of the veterans rode in wheelchairs. Some were accompanied by younger family members. Bundled up despite the springtime warmth of a day in May, they smiled and waved to the people who stood five-deep along the sidewalks; they waved to children sitting on their father's shoulders. Today, the veterans basked in the profound and openly proclaimed gratitude of the countrymen for whom they had fought.

Never mind that their pensions were nearly worthless.

Never mind that the pharmacies may not carry the medicines they needed.

Today they were heroes, in a country in desperate need of heroes.

The parade reached the end of Nevsky Prospect, turned to the right and dispersed into Palace Square, the vast open area between the Winter Palace and the General Staff Building where so much history had taken place, . . . and where today, families were waiting for grandmother and grandfather.

In the center of Palace Square stands the Alexander Column, a red granite column a hundred and fifty feet tall, cut from a cliff beside the Gulf of Finland. Atop this column stands the figure of an angel, who commemorates the Russian victory over Napolean's army in 1812. Consider for a moment: she is an angel, not an officer on horseback. She holds a cross in her hand, not a sword. Her other hand does not point toward the enemy, but upward toward heaven. She does not glare at the world with an aura of military glory, but bows her head with suffering and compassion.

On the 9th of May, 1995, the angel of St. Petersburg looked down upon her aging warriors, and upon the crowd that had come to congratulate them.

In ten years, many of the veterans will be gone. But their children, and the children of their children, whom they have taught to love their country, to loathe war, and to cherish peace, will always remember them.

———————

What can we learn—we who always fought our wars "over there"—from people who ate dogs, cats, leather belts, library paste and sawdust, because their daily ration of 125 grams of bread guaranteed only prolonged weeks of dying?

What can we learn from Russians who lived in the valley of the shadow of death, in a city where the Soviet government had long ago closed the doors of their churches?

What can we learn from a school where a woman who wears ruffles between her medals is invited every year to teach history?

The people in the land of our former enemies, the people in the land of our former allies, have something precious to teach us. They know that honor, and respect, and gratitude should be part of every school's curriculum. They know that every kid needs a hero, not a Hollywood hero, not a TV hero, not a comic book hero; each girl and each boy needs a real hero.

The Russians understand, because of their own grim experience, that war will repeat itself all too often, unless the children know, in their hearts, that war is not an action video, not a TV thriller, not a re-playable computer game . . . but a cruel and mindless crime.

Chapter Ten

OUR DESTINIES

And so we approach the end of a small book on an enormous subject.

A few vignettes, then, from springtime in St. Petersburg, when the low apricot sun of winter climbs higher into the sky; and the sheet of ice across the Neva breaks into jagged gray chunks that sweep downstream toward the Gulf; and oaks three hundred years old, planted in the days of Peter the Great, put out their shiny green leaves. The parks throughout the city sprout with crocuses and baby carriages. As the days grow longer and stretch themselves into the evening, fathers stroll along the paths with their scampering children.

On Saturday, the 4th of May, 1996, the broad sandy beach below the stone walls of the Peter and Paul Fortress was crowded with people in bathing suits and bikinis. (Or at least, the bottoms of bikinis.) The sun, flexing his muscles, beamed down from a crystalline blue sky, so that we on the beach felt like butterflies stretching our wings after we had crawled out of our dark damp cocoons. Laughing men and women smacked a volleyball back and forth in high arches over a tattered net. Men wearing a variety of bathing suits ranging from bloomers to a thong stood along the fortress wall, where the sun-baked air was the warmest, some facing the stones, some leaning back against them, as they tanned their burly chests, their bellies, and their bottoms.

Other people sat at the water's edge: a mother read a book while her child dug in the sand; teenage sweethearts held hands as they sat quietly on a towel and stretched their feet, in socks and nylons, toward the river; a girl wearing a pink bikini, and a pair of Walkman headphones, faced the sun sparkling on the river and danced her own private, graceful Rite of Spring.

No one swam. The ice on the river had washed away a week ago, and now the ice from Lake Ladoga, forty-six miles upstream, was drift-ing past. Beneath the shouts from the volleyball net, and the murmurs of the sun worshippers, I could hear another sound: a faint musical clinking from the river as the chunks of ice jostled with each other on their journey to the sea.

THE REVENGE OF THE BLACK BANANA

It was a warm evening in spring, and for the first time in half a year, I was able to sleep with the window open. Suddenly I was blasted awake! . . . by the five hundredth car alarm that had shattered my sleep since the day I moved in. I no longer sat bolt upright in bed; I now bur-ied my head beneath the pillow and waited for the berserk, unearthly wailing to stop.

But this car alarm shrieked and buzzed and burped for several min-utes, then it began to repeat through its cycle of howls. Better if some-one did steal the car, then the damn alarm would. . . . It stopped. I groaned with relief, and began to lift the pillow, when it started again! While fierce curses and vile imprecations yowled in my brain, the screaming gizmo in the courtyard turned OFF and ON and OFF and ON, as if, like the chirping of a five-ton cricket, it would continue all night.

I dragged myself out of bed and staggered across the dark room to the window. Peering down six stories—through the first tiny leaves on the maples—I discovered that there *was* a reason for the alarm: in the glow of the auto repair shop lamp, the car's owner was standing near a front fender, testing his little hand-held remote control unit. With a mere touch of his thumb, he turned the alarm ON, and then OFF, and then ON, and . . .

On the table beside the window, next to the rusty hotplate which had served as my "stove" all winter, lay two black bananas. When I had bought the original bunch at the market, the bananas had been over-ripe. Though I had eaten a banana a day, these last two had passed beyond the threshold point at which bananas become pure goosh. The trash was collected from my room once a week, and with several days to go, this pair had become progressively blacker.

My hand reached for the black bananas. With the shrewd cunning of a longsuffering peasant who had just sniffed the first scent of revenge, I understood that I could not toss them down from my own window, for I might be discovered.

Quickly I put on my robe, opened my door and glanced up and down the long dark empty corridor. Then I hurried with a mix of seething rage and rising excitement up the hallway to the Ladies' Room at the end. A quick faint knock, and then I entered the dark room and closed the door quietly behind me. Without turning on the light, I crossed with bare feet on the cool tile floor to the window—a dark window like dozens of other dark windows in the building—and peered down . . . with great pleasure, for I was now directly above the oblivious bonehead who was still testing (Please don't stop!) his wailing, beeping, burping car alarm.

Moving with silent stealth, I unlocked and slowly swung open the big old-fashioned window; cool springtime air, lightly scented by blossoming trees, drifted into the dank bathroom. I broke the stem of one black banana from the stem of the other. Then I cocked my hand as if I were throwing a dart at a bull's eye . . . and launched my missile. I did so quickly, with no estimation of elevation, no calculation of trajectory; my arm did it all by instinct.

And did it perfectly. That banana must have really been moving after its gravitational acceleration through a drop of six floors, for when it hit the roof of the car—smack-dab in the middle of the roof!— it splattered with an almost explosive force that gave me great satisfaction.

The high-tech Neanderthal with his hand-held gizmo jumped back about five feet and ducked, . . . then he slowly stood up and wiped his hand across his shirt. Staring at his palm in the glow of the lamp, he saw what he probably thought was lungs turned into pulp by a shrapnel wound.

Looking now at his car, he discovered the remnants of a banana peel on its roof. He had sufficient presence of mind to look up, though he could not see me standing just slightly back from the dark window, grinning with peasant glee.

And then—tra la!—he thumbed the button one more time, and the car alarm stopped in mid-wail. Silence . . . tentatively . . . filled the courtyard.

Concerned, no doubt, and justifiably so, that after the banana, a coffee cup might descend from the sky, and then perhaps a piano, Mister Lobotomy got into his car, roared its engine and scurried off. I *was* a bit sorry, for my adrenaline level was at such a point that I could easily have ripped a radiator off the bathroom wall, then launched it with absolute precision.

I closed the window, peered out the bathroom door, then slunk along the dark corridor to my room. I set the second banana back on its table, ready for the next skirmish.

But I heard nothing more, before I drifted off to sleep, than the yowl of a cat with a case of springtime hormones . . . . and the ethereal chimes of the cathedral, bestowing their gentle benediction on the slumbering city of St. Petersburg.

THE CHILDREN'S FESTIVAL

On the first of June, 1996, a Saturday of jubilant sunshine, children and their parents gathered in Palace Square for an event that had no political purpose, no historical purpose, no economic purpose. During the day-long Children's Festival, clowns and musicians appeared on a stage in front of the Winter Palace and entertained a crowd of thousands. They were joined by choruses and dance troops from schools around the city, so that most of the people performing were kids. The Square itself bustled with activity: small children bounced in carnival houses made of pumped-up cushions of air; older kids played basketball on temporary street courts. Families waited in long snaking lines for ice cream and balloons.

The city fathers handed out boxes of chalk, so the kids could draw on the smooth concrete pavement. Toddlers doodled, while older kids drew rabbits and daisies and rainbows. Thus the pavement which the tzar's carriage had once crossed, the pavement from which Russia's armies had marched to the disaster of the First World War, the pavement across which Lenin's Red Guard had advanced in darkness on the night they captured the Winter Palace, the pavement which had been blasted and pocked and shattered by Hitler's bombs, and the pavement which for half a century had been Ground Zero, became on this day an easel for the children who will take their city into the twenty-first century.

Out toward the edge of Palace Square, far from the stage, where there was plenty of space for a picture, a girl wearing blue jeans and sneakers, her blond hair in a braid, drew a large pastel-blue earth with yellow lines of latitude and longitude. Standing on top of this world are a boy and a girl holding hands. (The girl wears a dress, and a bow in her hair.) Between their feet, a rising sun peeks over the horizon.

The girl and boy stand on top of this globe, this world, this planet, as if they live not in a neighborhood, not just in St. Petersburg, nor even in Russia; they are citizens of the world.

Above them, above their earth and rising sun, the teenage artist chalked in red the Russian word LYUBOV.

In English, LOVE. What sort of love? Between boy and girl? Between Peoples of the world? I leave that for her generation to determine.

Almost without exception, the children in Palace Square were well-dressed, with bows, baseball caps and bright dresses, with hand-knit sweaters and shiny shoes, as if their parents were announcing to the world, "You see, despite all, our children are beautiful."

———————

Russia, a European-Asian country that spans much of a continent, is forever peripheral, forever preponderant. Though she lives at the distant edge of Europe, her heavy steps can shake every European floorboard. The pulse of her economy can be read on tickertapes in New York, and the success or failure of her farmers can effect the price of wheat in Lincoln, Nebraska. She bids good night to Norway as she bids good morning to Alaska.

Should you decide that on your next vacation, instead of barbequing burgers in the back yard with Uncle Bob in Baltimore, you would rather visit St. Petersburg, be forewarned, for almost certainly:

you will fall in love;

your heart will weep as it has never wept before;

your heart will open to the children: mischievous, proud, delightfully polite, talented children;

you will be given gifts, you will be loaded with gifts, more gifts than you can possibly fit into your suitcase, by people for whom a bunch of bananas is a major purchase;

you will hear music with your soul as you never heard it before;

despite your insistence that ballet is for sissies, you will agree to go to the theater, and you will be entranced;

you will be blessed by a Russian grandmother, whether you deserve it or not;

you will shake the hand of a man who speaks no English, but whose firm handshake and earnest eyes you will never forget;

you will come to understand that you are responsible for people beyond your own family, beyond your own town, beyond your own fruited plain from sea to shining sea;

you will smell the incense and hear the strange Orthodox words, as you, your heart brimming, bow your head and say a prayer;

and when you return home, you will look at your country, your neighbors, and yourself with entirely new eyes.

For better or for worse, whether we like it or not, our destinies are linked forever.

Postscript

January, 1999. The first month of the last year of the millennium. All of the world is preparing for New Year's Eve a year from now. Planning where they will be, planning who they will be with.

Except the Russians. Who, locked back in the Thirties, look at us in the distant Nineties. They watch the antics of frivolous wastrels, who claim to know all the answers. Do they envy us? You bet. Are they angry with us? Absolutely. Did we lose a good friend, or who might have been the best of friends, had we invited them? Yes, we most certainly did lose the best possible friends we could have had.

In 1989, the Soviets endured the tragedy of losing almost everything they believed in. And in 1989, the Russians had the courage to begin life anew. It was a strange, contradictory life, frightening, exhausting, and one that brought little reward.

Fledgling democrats survived an attempted Communist coup in 1991. The peaceful Russian people remained peaceful, while they watched the last antics of their old government.

They watched a band of Russian thieves rob the nation of goods, of money, of every last scrap of integrity. Meanwhile, they themselves sold potatoes on the street, and vegetables from the family garden, and books from the bookshelves at home, and shoes and boots that no one wore anymore, and leftover plumbing fixtures, and *VOGUE* and *MARIE CLAIRE* with Russian text, and a song on a violin.

They repaired their churches, carrying themselves buckets of fresh cement on a Sunday afternoon to smooth the cracked and sunken floor of the central aisle. They raised the money for blue paint, and white, and then they painted. They bought candles, they bought incense. And in a newborn church, packed shoulder to shoulder, they heard the ancient words spoken in the ancient language, and they prayed in their hearts as only people who have at last been given freedom can pray.

They tried to master this new thing called *capitalism*, which they had been taught to mistrust and hate. And they watched "investors" from other countries put money into the Russian stock market, and into some businesses. They watched these "investors"; and they heard tales of great profits; and then they watched the "investors" pull their money out quickly when the market looked "shaky". And they learned that the foreign investors were just another band of thieves.

Meanwhile, back at the ranch in Los Angeles, we watched O.J. Meanwhile, back at the ranch in Washington, we learned about Monica. Meanwhile, back at the ranch in Salt Lake City, we discovered bribes to the Olympic Committee.

I could go on, but you get my drift. We blew it. We, the island, blew it with them, the continent between Europe and Asia. Maybe, dude, we just passed to them the torch of Manifest Destiny.

Watch what they'll do with it. Their slowly growing nation won't be Wall Street. It won't be Hollywood. In the tapestry of Russian sound, soon to come our way from Russian composers, and filmmakers, and balladeers, we shall hear the voice of Peter the Great, as one voice among many, but that voice will clearly be Peter's. We shall hear the voice of a priest, an ancient voice, a strong voice. We shall hear the voice of a woman, of many, many women, from Murmansk and from St. Petersburg and from Tula and Ulyanovsk and from villages where the main dish is rice and goat, and her voice, their voices, shall speak with the power of the ocean tide, bearing ships from the harbor to the sea.

Pushkin is waiting. For the next poet.
Tolstoy is waiting, for the next great storyteller.
Dostoyevsky is waiting, for the next great portraitist.
Tchaikovsky is waiting, for the next sugarplum fairy.
And they will not be disappointed.

While we, back at the tailgate party, offer libations to the gods Mammon, Bacchus, and Web.

Where will I be on New Year's Eve, at the threshold of the new millennium?

Not on Times Square. Not on the International Dateline. Not in Greenwich, England, standing astride the white stripe.

I hope, with all my heart, to be in a small, stuffy, (perhaps frigid, perhaps overheated,) book-filled apartment, eating bread and pickled mushrooms, and drinking a bit more than my quota of vodka, and listening,

listening,

to voices which I understand, though their language I often do not,

for these voices speak of peace, after a century of wars;

and of schools for their children, as precious and as beautiful and as clever as children can be, but who need a chance, just a fair chance in the world;

and these voices speak of a river filled with poison, of a lake nearly dead;

they speak of freedom as a prisoner speaks of freedom,

they speak of hunger and sickness and death as a prisoner speaks of hunger and sickness and death.

Someone will hear them. Someone in Russia, as the clock ticks toward midnight on New Year's Eve, December 31, 1999, will hear those voices, hoping, lamenting, praying, cursing with rage. There will be many such listeners. Millions of them, and their average age will be about nineteen years old. The average age, in the old days, of soldiers sent to Vietnam, to Afghanistan. But now, these kids, these beautiful Russian kids, will begin to show the world the real Russia. Talented, wary, motivated, suspicious, graceful, and ingenious in unexpected ways, they will follow neither Stalin's lead, nor Lenin's, nor the tzars', nor will they worship at the foot of Western prophets. They will invent their own nation, and they will do it with talent, with hope, with compassion, and with vigor.

John Slade holds a Doctorate in Comparative Literature from Stanford University and a Masters in Education from the University of Vermont.

He has taught high school and college English for twenty-five years, in the United States, on St. Croix in the Caribbean, in Norway, and in Russia.

Other books by John Slade

DANCING WITH SAMUEL

A JOURNEY OUT OF DARKNESS

HERBERT'S MOUNTAIN

GOOD MORNING, DADDY!

A DREAM SEEDED IN THE EARTH

CHILDREN OF THE SUN

Available from
WOODGATE INTERNATIONAL
P.O. Box 190
Woodgate, New York 13494

315-392-4508